MEDIUM CHILL

Edited by: Dr. Rhonda Baughman

Issue 1 is for:
Canton, OH: Shawn Wenzel, Mike Fite
Massillon, OH: Joan Humphrey

CONTENTS

F

by Mike Polnik

Fuck you. The words went through the air, not like a normal sound of human. Not the way a mother calls her child in for dinner. Not like a coach yells for a wrestler to pull the leg in. No, this fuck you, it moved through the air like a haymaker; void of the technique and timing of a left hook by Joe Frazier. It moved through the air like a battering ram. The sound would have hit the cortex at the precise moment that fist struck the jaw line. The words struck, then stuck, in the mind as the punch smashed face. Both strikes, perhaps representative of the years of hell this young man has gone through. The years of agony from little words of "*stupid*" and "*idiot*" to the void of language. Those moments when he would look up from the mat and see the empty space where his hero wasn't, yet again. Very few people understand that the silence of no words can be more painful that the venom of those heard. At least being told he was dumb meant he wasn't alone again. He didn't have to answer the door for bill collectors or pretend he wasn't alone with his sister when the family called "to say hi."

Fuck you. This time. This fucking time. It was it. The pain was there. And like all scars, they heal but still reshape the future. He had those as well. Those scars from the belt. The buckle, it hurt the worst. He always knew when the hand went from the beer can down to the front of his pants, the belt was coming.

Fuck you. He would take it. Every time he would stand there and take the abuse. Then, like a sad replay of a movie most people watch horrified, he would walk to school with long sleeve shirts in the summer. Of course, he was hot and of course, he wasn't dumb. He heard all the teasing. He knew it was because of the way he dressed and acted. Always jumpy and just a little bit off. Never enough to be noticed by anyone. Yet, enough that after the police investigation all those in life would gather together to act as if they all noticed. Yes, they would marvel at their perceptive ability and trade stories to just increase the drama of the unifying small talk that often occurs when people fail to see what's in front of them and want to feel better about missing it.

Fuck you. The years of torment, they didn't build like some metaphor into a volcano. No. They increased the wet and dampness of his soul. Everyday acting full to avoid not having money. Everyday acting busy to avoid the after school activities. Hell, every field trip he would wander around the outside because having more for the gift shop was never real. He knew the bus driver very well.

Fuck you. His sister was always safe. He made sure of it. He would distract dad on those drunk nights. He would even make up stories of failures to draw the ire of him to avoid any chance of hurting her. He would take it all in, then hold her as she tried to sleep. More than once, he would hold her head with one hand and wipe blood from his nose onto his shirt with the other. More than once, he would then lay still and be afraid to breathe – the noise of this basic function might remind the evil stumbling in the hallway that there was still an opportunity to increase the hell. Once the snoring roared thought the house, like the reverse of the alarm horn that sounded when a tornado came near, this loud and penetrating sound meant peace. He passed out. It was time to walk down the hall to try to get some homework done.

Fuck you. He saw the look. That night, the look moved. That fucking look. That fucking empty stare of a subhuman sperm donor who had to prove his back injury was real every day at the bar. That fucking look. When it came, it was different. It meant another type of pain was coming. When the hand went in the front of the pants and the belt buckle was undone, it meant pain was coming. When the belt didn't begin to slide out of the loops and the hand slowly turned into a tool to move the zipper; that pain was worse. It didn't happen often. Though, it is a sad reality that he even had to use terms like often in regards to these moments. It is even sadder that those few moments of agony would even have to be discussed in a court room. The touching was where his soul died. When that Thursday night happened and he turned to her sitting on the couch doing her homework, that look and the movement of the hands. There will never be a way to know if the belt was being removed or not. What was known was that the devil was arriving.

Fuck you. It was as if cat piss had become verbal. The pungent stench of cat piss that filled the air and made its way into his mind as his fist crashed into his jaw. The punch was beautiful. Not in technique. Not in precision. Not even in some warped sense of justice. It was beautiful in that it was the expression of the protector. The young man doing what mothers and fathers were to do. As it crashed into his jaw, the feel of the stubble was rough as slipping on the driveway. The first three knuckles of youth, rage, and determination met the façade of a man who did not deserve the love of the children.

Fuck you. He fell. Not as a tree in the woods. He fell like the wet trash bags that were thrown into the street every Monday morning. The next moment would come fast. He knew that. Not in the way he would try to stand up, but in the way that nothing was ever going to be the same in their lives again. Right or wrong, good or bad, didn't play into the moment. Existential change. That was swift and true. As the old man drew up a knee, as those old jeans slid like a snake to bring the evil upright....

Fuck you. A second blow was struck with the knee right to the nose. The very knee that was scraped so many times as he tried to teach himself how to ride a bike. The same knee that would move up and down in that rhythmic dance of peddling that would transport him away from home and to the back of the body shop where he could sit and pray, fumbling through a rosary for protection then thinking the lack of divine help was tied to his inability to recite it properly. This knee that knelt during mass, that bumped into the top of desk at school, and was toughened from wrestling practice was an instrument of a position. It was not a Muay Thai technique, though many would marvel at its force and speed. It was the second part of a two word statement from a boy to a man. It was the end of an era. It was the end of a story. It was also the password. Like a masonic password to enter into lodge, it entered the family into a new world. It entered his sister into his aunt's house in Arizona. It entered his father into jail. It entered him into a foster family that was good enough, but ultimately entered him into the United States Marine Corps. The two words he spoke that night. *Fuck. You.* Aligned with the dual destructive force of a brother who loved his sister more than safety.

Fuck you. His glass stuck another as the mission was over and they were safe. He sat in a barrack drinking with his best friend. They went though basic together and defended his sister in the war. As he retold this story for the first time, his friend bonded with him saying: "my old was an asshole, too." The bond was complete. The hell was normalized and set down into the soul as a cornerstone to his resolution to build himself into a man. He was his own man. He was an uncle to his beautiful two nieces that sent him cards with pictures colored from a chain restaurant. Even years later as he sat at a small kitchen table, a baby slamming little pasta circles into a tray, his wife smiled and told him that the envelop for his admission into college sat in his hands still dirty from fixing cars. He looked at her, got a tear and tasted salt again – a familiar sensation – he opened it to see his opportunity unfold in front of his battle hardened eyes. He sat back, smiled from the area of his mouth his wife didn't know moved up and thought and knew and said …

I did it.

Fuck you.

"I did it."

Family iz Forever
by Jaime Bunnell

I vault the short wall that separates a dinette from the kitchen and squeeze two shots from my pistol into the chest of the man hidden there. He slumps back against the dishwasher. I check my clip, discard the handgun, and pick up the AR15 he was firing. "Thanks," I whisper to him, knowing he can't hear me anymore.

I pin myself against the center island and hit my radio.

"One down in the kitchen," I say loud enough my team can hear, but not enough to jeopardize my position. The granite countertops are an especially nice touch to this kitchen. The lighting is just so that it reflects off the polished surface and creates a bloom in your eye. There's a half-eaten sandwich on the counter, complete with some kettle chips, a pickle, and an empty beer glass.

"I could really go for a beer," I whisper into the radio, to my partner.

"I'll buy you two after it's over," he calls back over the radio. "Let's wrap this up."

"One sec."

Through the window, I catch a hint of movement in the driveway. I swear it's the figure of a woman, obscured by the branches. I lean against the countertop, trying to get a better view, but the sunlight plays through the branches, casting warm reds and brassy oranges across the window.

***

"What do you think?" my mother asked with a slow spin. It's a bronze, asymmetric blouse with big swirls of rust and dark jade. Autumn as clothing.

"I love it, mom."

"It's a little thin," she added. She pulled the bottom of the shirt out from her waist and stared at it. Her face wrinkled slightly. "I can see the floor through it."

"Just wear a cami under it," I offered. "I'll grab you one." I spun and headed through the racks before she could protest. When I returned with two - one wine and the other forest - my life shattered to pieces against the ground around my mother, collapsed there in the dressing room.

We joked, after she left the ER, that it was the most expensive blouse she'd ever shoplifted.

***

"Jax," a voice crackles through my earpiece. I jolt back to the kitchen and crouch down, cheeks warm from leaving my back exposed in the middle of a breach. "Converge on the office in the back of the house. Last two hostiles are there."

"Roger that." With my rifle at the ready, I stand and head to the corridor to rendezvous with my partner, Marcus. I've never seen this guy lose his cool in the five years we've been working together - our de facto raid leader. I smile. "Ready to -"

"Shit," he says and shoves me. I slam back into the hallway and watch a combat knife sail past us and bury its blade deep into the wall. Marcus falls against the opposite wall and fires off a three-round burst at the man down the hall. The bullets glide through his head and a red mist explodes on the closed door behind him.

"Thanks."

"Hey, no big deal," Marcus says as he switched clips. "Consider it payback for saving me from that perp a few weeks ago."

"That was real life, though."

"You think this is a game?" He smirks and I laugh.

"All right," he says, "we kick open that door and put down the last shit-head and get outta here." He starts down the hallway, "Ricky and Nesbit will be here in five to evac." The door to the office erupts in splinters against Marcus' boot. We rush into to the room and I hope we're not too late.

On the far side, our last hostile reclines in a high-back office chair. The Kevlar vest almost hides the truth, but her raven ringlets and bright cheeks give her away. She smiles as we train our rifles to her head. "Too late," she gestures at the desk, "you lose."

On the desk that separates us, a large, gray box sits with its lid open. I glance in to see its display tick down to 0:00 as she laughs.

"Fuck," I sigh. I toss the controller on the sofa beside me and slide off my headset. The screen fades to black as *Blue Team wins* haunts the top of the it and match stats fade in below. *Rating change: -150.* "Well," I say to the T.V., "there goes a whole afternoon of wins."

I check the window one last time, my mind holding on to the shadowy unknown that easily cost us the match. "You spent at least ten seconds looking out this damn window, Jackson," I say to my reflection in the glass, "ten seconds in a real crisis would've gotten someone killed."

There, in the driveway, stands a memory from my past.

"Fuck."

My phone chirps from the end table and I glance at the notification: *Where you at Jax?* I pick up the headset and brace myself. "I gotta bail, Mark"

"Dude! Come on!" His voice reminds me of my wife's after she's thrown the Friday crossword, half completed, into the trash. "I thought we were good for an afternoon of gaming?"

"Yeah," I offer with a dejected olive branch, "I thought so to. But, now my mom is here and I gotta deal with her."

"You told me your mom died when you were in high school." Mark's voice is full of twisting gears and dead ends.

"Yeah," I say, "look, it's complicated." I search the den for anything extra to offer him. On the mantle, a photograph of my mother and I sits framed in a clean-edged, dark frame. We're standing on our old front porch and I'm dressed in a suit I borrowed from my father's closet to take my girlfriend to prom. It was the same year my father moved out and only a month after I'd come out to my mom. Every time I look at her in the photo, I try to see if I can tell that the cancer was already reducing her body to wreckage.

I never can.

***

My head deep in the bowels of the fridge, I slide the orange juice to the side - for the third time - and peek behind it. There's still nothing there. "Hey Abby?" I say to my wife, "where's the beer?"

"It should be in there … unless you drank it all," she replies.

"I don't think I drank it all." I count on my fingers the matches I played online with Mark. It didn't feel like a six pack, but maybe it was. I slide the milk, just to be sure. "Damn."

"It's barely three o'clock," Abby says, "I'll run out after dinner and get a growler of something."

I sigh and close the door. "I was just hoping to have a beer while I deal with this." Abby glances across the top of her book with accusing eyes. *With what,* they say. "Mom's outside."

"Jackson?" Abby eases closed the book she's reading.

"I got it," I wave my hand, "go back to your book."

"Jackson Marie," her voice is bold. I stop with the front door cracked open. Through the screen door, I can see my mother waiting. She never comes all the way up to the porch. She prefers to wait in the driveway, near the trees. Last time, she said she felt like Abby didn't like her visiting.

"You know I don't like it when you call me that." I say, not moving my eyes from the driveway. "My mother called me that when I was little and -"

"Well, sometimes it seems like I need to treat you like a child to get you to pay attention to what I'm saying." When she's angry, she likes to bring up previous disputes. I forgive her this because I know I can be a real bitch too. "I think you need to head back into the den and spend time playing your war game with Mark. Your mom will understand. She'll leave eventually if you just let her be."

"I said I got this." I slam the door harder than I intend.

***

"Mom. You're not supposed to be here." The words leave my mouth but they make no sense. Her skin is gray, pulled taut against her bones. She stares at me through glossy, milky marbles that never blink. "I thought we talked about this?"

A softball sized clump of wet dirt falls from her shoulder and splats against the driveway, ruining the moment of silence we enjoy. "You should call your father," her words are dry and dusty and ten years stale.

I let out a heavy breath before realizing it might come across insulting. "I don't have anything to say to him."

"He needs you." A small puddle of viscous liquid pools around her right foot. It sits, as unmoved as me. It's a deep green, almost black, the kind that imbibes horror and retching at a glance. It's the words my father spat on the ground between us before that prom picture was taken. *No daughter of mine.*

Indeed.

Milestones would pass like mile markers along the highways that now separate us - graduation, mom's death, college, police academy, marriage. They passed by until the fog of war slowly obscured him so much it was almost impossible to see him. One morning, it had swallowed him up and I was an orphan.

"No," I say, "if he needed me, he wouldn't have acted the way he did. He'd try to call. He -"

Some of her forearm pulls away from the bone and splashes into the black puddle beneath her feet. "I won't leave until you promise to go see him."

***

It's not the first time she'd done this. That was my junior year. Two years into a nursing program I absolutely hated, she showed up one night. I been out drinking with a sorority friend who would eventually become my wife.

On my way back to my dorm, I found my mother near the quad sitting on a bench in the moonlight. She was still fairly fresh, for a dead person. Her skin had lost its shine, her hair drier and frizzy, her eyes just slightly sunken and milky. But still very much my mother.

"What the fuck," I said and tried to blink away what I was seeing. "Why … How are you even here?"

"I don't know," she said, "But, why are you here?"

"What?"

She sat vacant for a moment. Some kind of dark liquid began to ooze from the corner of her eye. "What happened to law enforcement? Ever since you were a little girl, you wanted to be a police officer."

"I changed my mind. I want to help people."

She tilts her head, her vertebrae grind against each other in defiance. "When the neighborhood kids wanted to play cops and robbers, you demanded to be the cop. You even beat-up Aaron that time he wouldn't let you play a cop." My mother's mouth hung open for a moment and a laugh like sandpaper scoured the air between us.

"Those were just games. This is serious."

"Jackson Marie, you can't save me." I opened my mouth to argue, but she interrupted before I spoke, "And you'd make a fine police officer."

I stared out across the quad for a minute. "Maybe." I turned back to my mother, but she was gone.

I threw up on the sidewalk in front of me.

***

"Jackson," my wife's words stomp across the pavement, her annoyance buried deep in her tone.

"Abbigail!" my mother's face would've lit up, if it wasn't rotting off her skull. Instead, my wife's name drips from her lips in dry, guttural hoarseness. "You haven't changed a bit. Just as beautiful as your wedding day."

"Jackson," Abby repeats herself, "you really shouldn't be out here, especially in the middle of a Saturday afternoon." She gestures towards the neighbors' houses. "What if our neighbors -"

"It's no big deal," I offer, trying to disarm the minefield scattered between us.

My mother cocks her head to the side, slowly crawling through her distant and dissolving memories - much like the worms literally crawling through the remains of her mind. She groans - her default response to any and all stimulus - and returns her head upright.

"We weren't talking about you," I offer.

"Stop!" Abby's words are loud and aggressive. As if jarred by them, some dirt shakes loose from my mother's shoulder and skitters down the torn, faded remnants of the blouse she wore to her funeral. "While I love your mother, she needs to leave." She turns away from me and adds, "Now." With heavy steps, she heads back into our house.

"I've upset her," my mother words fall between us flat and apathetic.

"No, mom. It's fine," I say.

"Oh Jackson, you never could lie to me very well." She stares over my shoulder, lost in some distant sunset. A bit of vaguely green liquid pools at the corner of her mouth threatening to bungee towards the ground below.

She never blinks. I think that's what bothers me most. I could push past the whole arisen dead thing if she'd blink. Ever. But the endless, insistent darkness of her eyes feels like roaches crawling along my arms just below the skin.

"Call your father," she says, returning suddenly from torpor.

"No, mom," I say. "We've talked about this. I'm not putting myself through that shit again."

"People change."

"I promise he hasn't."

"You'll regret it when he's gone." She reaches her hand out towards mine. Her nails are chipped and jagged, the underside of each one coated in grayish brown dirt. She would never stand for these nails when I was younger and she was more alive.

Every couple months, at the threat of combat, she would drag me to her salon. I like to keep my nails trimmed, not letting but a hint of white crescent peek out at the edges. Still, I let my mother have this moment with her daughter. Even now, Abby complains that I "waste money on that nail tech when it's just going to chip off at work anyway."

"Jackson?" my mother pulls me back to the present.

"Regret what? Not giving him another chance to shit on my life?" The words are sharper than I intend and my mother winces, if zombies can. "Maybe he can visit from time to time and remind me just how much of an abomination I am?" My emotions swell up at the edges of my eyes, threatening to streak down my cheeks and roll across my chin. I throw up on the driveway in front of me.

When I look up, she's gone. "Fine!" I shout into the afternoon. "I'll call him!"

***

"Hello," a woman's voice answers. Her voice has a rasp of cigarettes and whiskey. A perfect compliment to him.

"Is Richard there?" I grind my teeth to stifle a scream. I pace toward the house and settle under the shade of the porch.

She's silent, then "Who is this?" Her words are terse, nearly cut short. She sniffles.

"It's his daughter, Jackson." I force the words through my teeth.

"The lesbian?"

"What the fuck? Look, can you just put him on the phone?"

"He drank his last shot a few months ago, hun." I hear her sip, probably whiskey, and slam it against a table.

"I don't care if he quit drinking. I -"

"Ain't what I said, dyke." The phone falls silent. I pull it away from my ear to confirm she hung up on me.

I turn back towards the driveway, arms open, "I tried mom. I tr -" But my mother isn't there to meet my words. Instead, a middle-aged man - at least what remains of him - stands, a long-empty bottle of whiskey in his left hand. His right, not with him. The same taut skin and vacant expression. "Where'd mom go?"

"Passed her on the way in," my father says. "Sounded like she wasn't coming back."

It's over. I think.
by Mike Hammer

"First of all, take my name off your answering machine message. I no longer live with you and I will never again live with you. Second, just so you know, I am going out with my ex-girlfriend tonight. I don't mean a girl who was a co-worker friend of mine, that kind of girlfriend, I mean my ex-girlfriend who I used to date and fuck. We are going to her place. We will not be playing Parcheesi or Trivial Pursuit, we will be fucking. I will be cumming all over her face and I will not be thinking of you at all as she licks my pussy clean. Who even has an answering machine anymore?" (Laughter)

"I will be cumming loudly and often. That is certainly something I have never done with you. Which is part of the reason I am never coming back. You called my dad an 'old drunk,' and I don't want to be with someone who disrespects my family. You can call me your whore, when we are alone. It's true that my nickname among past lovers was 'the sex goddess' and I wrenched every inch of satisfaction out of them using the naughtiest tricks possible, but I will not have you disrespect my family. I have never said a word about your aunt who overextends her credit cards, can't keep a job and keeps getting married again and again, like a new man will save her. I never said anything about your cousins who can't keep their legs closed and have babies all over the place and aren't even entirely sure who the fathers are. I don't say jack about your stripper sisters, who do more than is legal in the private rooms of those small, shitty clubs. So you cannot disrespect my father and expect me to stay with you. Whatever my father has or hasn't done he has done it to me and my family, not to you. You do not have the right to insert yourself into my affairs." (Tongue clicks)

"I would have been your sex goddess forever. I would have been the best thing you ever had, but you could not respect me. Silence is golden, you son of a bitch. But I will not be silent tonight. I will be going loud and long and hard. And you will never get to have me as your whore ever again. I will be someone else's whore. I will be the goddess for men, real men, who value me." (Muffled)

"Baby, come and kiss me. You better save this answering machine message you prick, this is the last time you will hear me cum. My girl is gonna make me cum on your answering machine. I will moan and I will cum all over her fingers as you listen and your cock gets big and hard, and there will be nobody there to lick it and suck it and drain it. Nobody there. I'm not coming back to you. You lost the sexiest goddess in the city and it's your own fault. Make me cum, oh God, my pussy's so wet, oh God. I'm going to fuck the phone and cum all over it, I'm going to yell into it and you're going to jerk off to me, I know you are." (Moans)

Pretty Please
by Dr. Rhonda Baughman

"Your request for pretty please has been denied," I say with a sunny smile.

I look at Jimmy. Jimmy looks at me. I continue to smile. Jimmy offers a tentative movement of lips. I stop smiling. And Jimmy stops attempting to. It's a sunless day for dear Jimmy.

"I'm joking, Jimbo. I just find it strange everyone here says 'pretty please' all the time, don't you?"

"Yes, Ma'm."

"Jimmy, you don't have to agree with me just to agree. You can have your very own opinion, you know."

Jimmy nods agreeably. I sigh and return the documents he came for, now signed. Jimmy's expression doesn't change.

"If it's within our budget and time constraints, I will almost certainly agree to it. On the other hand, if we can't afford it and have little to no time to implement effectively, I will deny the request. This makes sense, right? See why you don't have to say 'pretty please'?"

"Yes, Ma'm," Jimmy says, obviously with little comprehension of what I've said.

I sigh again. It's impossible not to here.

"Thanks, Jimmy. And keep up the good work."

He offers the expected 'Yes, Ma'm' once again before departure.

I look around at my windowless little bunker of an office, with a mind to knock out some of the fluorescent lights and install ... nothing. The less lights, the better – an ambiance to create a feeling of comfort and nostal -

My email boops.

Dear Dr. Traylebb: Can you please, pretty please, conduct a meeting on ...

And I stop reading. My eyes begin to water – whether from the lights, my interrupted reverie about the lights, or the fact that someone, yet again, has uttered the vile phrase 'pretty please' will remain unknown. I squeeze them tight, massage my neck, reopen my eyes slowly – and decide, yes, it's the phrase and nothing more. The not-exactly-tears-but-close-at-this-point I can handle, but the oncoming headache, I cannot. I buzz the front desk - extension 753273. I know it well.

"Dan, hold my calls for ten minutes. I'm going out to have a smoke. Is there any aspirin where you are?"

"Sure thing, Dr. T. Be my pleasure," he says.

"Thanks. Did today's mail arrive?"

"That it did, Dr. T. Would you like for me to bring it to you?" Dan asks.

"Just leave it on my desk, Dan, with the drugs," I say.

"Will do. Whaddya say?"

"Pardon?" I ask.

"Whaddya say?" Dan asks again.

"What do you mean? I don't -"

"Pretty please!" he says merrily.

I am not saying this phrase. Ever.

"Yes, Dan. With a cherry on top."

… and refrain from adding *you little twit of too cheerful shit.*

Walking from my office, down the hallway, and a few more offices, several from which I can hear laughter and chatter, microwave beeps and, regrettably, the day's phrase of doom.

"Pretty please?" Barbara says, into her phone, as I continue my walk, a little faster now, toward the area I thought I was over, but as evidenced by this moment, certainly am not.

I light up the moment I'm outside in the smoker's area, inhale deeply, vow never to stop smoking again, note it really is a sunless day, and begin to sift through my thoughts – a jumble of corporate stock phrases and sanctimonious sayings. Every office has them. Every firm. Every sector. But the pithy *pretty please* was caught in my craw like no other chestnut hitherto. And obviously, there are plenty of truisms at my disposal, but 'pretty please'? *Please.*

A maintenance crewman emerges from his car, nods in my direction. I nod in return. He motions to my cigarette.

"You want one?" I ask him.

"Pretty please?" he says and I hand over the rest of the pack, breaking the vow from only moments ago.

"All yours, man," I say and head back to my office. The cigarette only helped the jiggling train in my head to jump its track.

It's nowhere near lunch, but the aspirin serve as appetizer, the coffee I wash them down with gone cold, like my shoulder, at the next person who dare walk into my office and -

"Dr. Traylebb!   Can you pretty please sign these purchase orders?" Barbara asks.

"Barbara, why has this phrase, 'pretty please', crept into the office lexicon like a plague?"

Barbara looks at me, and the light of recognition is not in her eyes.

My eyes wander to my office clock – it reads 0900. I've been here for less than an hour and I'm vaguely bothered that I note this.

"You do know what I mean, don't you, Barbara?" I ask, the edge in my voice clear, perhaps from an aspirin chip in my throat. I take a sip of water, gone warm like my cheeks. Barbara has not answered. She inches closer with the documents.

"Could you, pretty please, sign these?" she asks and the lights in my office dim slightly, due to either a power surge or the universe's recognition, I shall never know.

"You know, Barbara -" I start and decide to try a different tactic. I return her documents to her unsigned.

"I would prefer not to," I say, just betting my clock's time would no longer bother me and the sun came out somewhere.

<u>Remembering for Mikey</u>
by Mark Hines

Huffing too many aerosol cans fried Mikey's brain. That's my theory on how he wound up here, based on the similarities I've observed between him and the "cheap high" burn outs I knew while working in the prison system.

No one here really knows the full story of how such a young guy wound up as just another chronic patient living out life among the other psychotics who are all twice his age. The kid could've been my little brother; He's shy, not very good at communication, has to press for every word like he's stuttering; only he's not. He had been shot in the head several years before, though how or why remains a mystery to us all.

Considering all, Mikey does okay for himself. He's stable when on meds, and kind of fades into the woodwork when too many others are around, but at least he is willing to try and communicate his feelings with those people who have earned his trust, and he seems especially drawn to being my silent shadow as I go about my duties.

He is a follower. He tends to mimic the actions of others, though not so much for purposes of staff manipulation as just for something to be doing. You see, his IQ is probably somewhere around fifty or so, but I can tell it wasn't something he was born with. The gunshot wound to the head undoubtedly has a lot to do with it, but he greatly reminds me of guys I knew who burned out on huffing shit for some reason.

I talk to him a lot when I have time. His short term memory is intact, but his long term memory is utterly devastated. He doesn't know how old he is. He doesn't know how long he's been in here, but he can tell you the month and the year. He knows the name of the town where he grew up, but he can't tell you anything about who he was or what he did. Virtually nothing. Just little specifics here and there.

Last night at ten o'clock I found him laying on his back out in the middle of the lawn. I knew he was okay when I saw him move as I approached. I thought maybe he was imitating another resident who likes to play dead sometimes for attention, so I decided to show him that two could play at that game by simply walking up silently, laying down skull to skull 180 degrees from him, and playing dead with him. After about a minute, he craned his head up toward mine, so I did the same thing toward him, and we just kind of gave each other a genuinely mimicked look of, "So what the Hell are you doing?"

Are we dead yet?" I said, letting him know that I knew what was up because somebody else had just tried the same stunt an hour before.

He laughed a burnout laugh and answered, "Yeah...." He understood what I meant. We both looked back upward then, and found that neither one of us really felt like pulling ourselves up off of the ground, so we both just stayed there.

"No..." He said about ten seconds later, but it was softly spoken and had ring of sadness inflected into it. And then, "I don't know..." It just kind of faded from him; not depressed, not confused, not completely making sense, but somehow I knew what he meant by it.

I realized what he had done. He must have gotten depressed and acted it out on impulse by imitating another whom he'd see play dead, only to find that when he layed out beneath the canvas of the clear night sky it distracted him,and he forgot what he was doing. That would answer, "Yes... No... I don't know," as well as suggest sadness over something.

We just laid there silently for a couple more minutes, a burnout and his caretaker on the front lawn of a countryside psych ward, and we fell into the sky. After a few minutes of silence, I began to point out the Big Dipper star by star, showing him where to look, and how to see it for himself. Then I told him how to find Polaris, the North Star, and told him about how pirates and armies used to navigate land and sea by the constellations. He got a kick out of that, so I continued by pointing out the little dipper, star by star, and told him about how they emptied into each other as the world spun... This REALLY blew his mind. What blew my mind was when he began to speak more as he got more exited about learning what I was showing him, and the slur of his speech began to fade a little bit as we talked.

"I can see it! I can SEE it, Mark! I can see it!" Whole phrases now, where before was just slurred single words.

So I kept doing this, pointing out every

constellation I could remember, and showing him how to find star after star. He didn't know what he was accomplishing. He was so caught up in the moment, and I dared not let it slip away from him by letting him know.

Draco. Orion. Gemini. I pointed out whatever I could see in the sky, and he ate it up. I hated it when I had to admit that I didn't know of any more constellations. I had intentionally kept him talking.

For those few moments Mikey spoke to me without a slur, in phrases, in the voice of the young man he must have been before whatever accident had befallen him. I just laid there looking back and forth between his upside down face and the stars, and I dared not make him aware of what he was accomplishing, for it was obviously some kind of a fluke, and I didn't want him to be distracted and lose the clarity he had, and make all those images fall away from him. I didn't want him to lose those pieces of himself he had lost growing up. I didn't want him to wake up from whatever trance he was in only to find himself the same old slurred spoken, "fighting with each word," not understanding anything, even how old he is" kind of idiot again.

It was inevitable. The moment passed. Mikey went back to being the same old Mikey I knew, that young guy my own age who only had half a brain left and hated it. He went from being dead, to alive, then back to not really knowing just what he was for sure anymore. I saw it happen, man. For fifteen minutes Mikey was just like you and me before his brain got fried. I think I would have been better off never having seen it, though. Star by star I brought this guy back; he loved it, and he laughed his ass off, never realized what he had accomplished.

"I CAN SEE IT! I CAN SEE IT, MARK! I CAN SEE IT!"

It tears my heart out to know that even as vivid as those stars were last night, come two weeks from now he won't remember a single damn thing about it.

Meeting Someone New
by Mike Hammer

*From Texas to Ohio is too long a walk, even if it's
with someone you love. Five miles in the walk you
already want to do them in. – Damien Jurado*

I left her body on the side of the road, her neck
broken, buzzards swarming. It was a scorching day
in Texas, her skin would be gone soon I thought,
smiling. From Texas to Ohio is too long a walk,
even if it's with someone you love. Five miles in
the walk you already want to do them in.

The first time I killed someone with my bare
hands it felt exhilarating, it felt like a major
accomplishment. It was the final, ultimate, end to a
struggle between two people, and I was victorious.
This time I still enjoyed the snap of the neck – a
trumpet heralding the end – but there was no
exhilaration. It was becoming routine.

The snap only meant I could rest.

I felt this way especially after killing a woman
– because it was more of a nuisance, than an
activity. For some reason I thought Shannon and I
could make it from Texas to Ohio together and she
could amuse me. But that wasn't what happened.

When we were 50 miles north of Waco the car
broke down in a dust storm. Nobody was around
and we decided to walk North to the next town to
get some help. Walking, thinking about Ohio,
listening to Shannon yammer, I knew I couldn't

walk any farther with her. I was just imagining
what would happen if we had to walk all the way
to Ohio.

I didn't love her. She was fun and I liked her well
enough but I found myself reaching over and
grabbing her. I had grabbed her before, in plenty of
ways that she liked, so she didn't fight back and I
broke her neck easily. Like a fisherman peeling a
shrimp, that's how easy and routine and business-
like it had become – death.

Death is so easy. Five miles away from that car
I realized life is what is hard. Shannon certainly
expected a long life – but I took that from her,
easily. People expect riches, but others take that.
People want Easy Street, but they get the hard way
and they crumble 85 percent of the time, maybe
more. The majority of people I have known in this
world just buckle under and put up with what was
dropped on them. Not enough people have the
audacity and balls to go and drop shit on others,
but that's how you gotta do it.

I walked all day wondering if I would find
someone in the next town who could drop some
shit on me, someone who would challenge me,
somebody who knew enough to save their neck.
When I got into the town I went to the car parts
place and the mechanic tried to hustle me. I
showed him my Magnum. He showed me his
Remington. We became friends.

I decided not to go to Ohio.

Purdie Delores Benjaminson
by Dr. Rhonda Baughman

Purdie Delores Benjaminson always showed her clients what they wanted. Even if they didn't know they wanted it.

"Do you want to see more?"

"I'm not sure. What's it gonna cost me?" Jack asked.

"What do you think I am, boy? Some kinda whore?" Purdie Delores Benjaminson wiggled her fanny to the music.

"No, ma'am. I-I-I do ... want ... to see more."

"Well, then, why didn't you just say so?" She opened her blouse to reveal a beautiful pair of tentacles.

The boy screamed.

Security entered and took him away.

Purdie Delores Benjaminson laughed and removed the tentacles, rubbed her arms and shoulders. Her tentacles wiggled about, then calmed, became still. She kissed them, then returned them to their full, upright positions, and rebuttoned her blouse.

Purdie Delores Benjaminson yawned. "That boy will be back. He doesn't know what he wants but Purdie Delores Benjaminson sure does." Her tentacles wiggled again. "You boys is tired, too. How about we rest a bit and wait for him to return? They always do."

The tentacles snoozed. Soon Purdie Delores Benjaminson snoozed, too.

A knock woke her.

Purdie Delores Benjaminson yawned, stretched, patted her hair. "Yes?"

"Purdie Delores Benjaminson? Are you ... available?"

They always come back.

"Why, yes, baby. I sure am. Come on in."

"I didn't mean to scream like that earlier, Ms. Purdie. And I want to apologize. My-my name is Jack."

'That's all right, boy. Jack, I mean. I know you meant no harm." Purdie Delores Benjaminson licked her lips. "Sit down, rest a spell. Let Purdie Delores Benjaminson show you something."

"I-I'd like that, Ms. Purdie. I won't scream this time."

"I know you won't, baby." Purdie Delores Benjaminson shimmied and shook, twisted and swayed. "You want to see something now, sugar buns?" Purdie Delores Benjaminson smiled.

"Yes, ma'am, I would love to!" Jack trembled and sat back in the booth.

"Okay, then. You just be still, Jackie."

Purdie Delores Benjaminson showed him everything. Jack didn't scream this time.

"I told you boys he wouldn't scream."

Purdie removed a tentacle from Jack's mouth, and the other from Jack's pants. Jack fell forward, onto the floor. Security came in and took him away.

Purdie Delores Benjaminson attached her new tentacle, and wiped the gore from her face and neck with her sleeves. She had a pretty new blouse behind the booth for these predicaments.

36

"You boys get to see more than anyone who comes in here," Purdie Delores Benjaminson said to her tentacles. They wiggled about, happily entwined with the third addition, then calmed, became still. Purdie buttoned her top and called it an evening. She wanted to go home and acquaint herself with her new appendage. Besides, the weekend loomed and Purdie Delores Benjaminson need some rest - she still had more clients to see and more room under her blouse.

<u>Soul Wide Shut</u>
by Scott Mayer

I pondered the box I carelessly opened when I told
her I loved her
Those words
Those words flew from my mouth without a
thought
Paranoia set in
A deep throbbing from the center of my universe
made me flush
Knowing the time had come to get burned
Sweat swelled from the sewers of my palms
The brine evaporated into the unknown
Never to be seen again
And that box
Remains open
Unable to be shut

<u>To Take a Cup</u>
by Dr. Rhonda Baughman

The knock interrupts my earliest events, those needing to unfold in a timely manner or the risk of ruining my day's plans rises. I set my first cup of tea down, gently, into its saucer, next to my biscuit tin and sugar spoon. Number two is not ready yet, its water still readying to boil on the stove, bag or loose leaf not yet chosen.

Opening the door, I see his bright smile, and in his hand a flyer of some sort. His tone is smooth, vocal cords forming words about cookies and his daughter's troop. His foot blocks my ability to close the door, so instead I invite him in. The monkey chitters all the way through the foyer, the kitchen, the mudroom, and out the back door, to my fenced-in property, intent on this sale. I know he'll say *No* to my offer of a cup of tea, and anyway, it's mine. All mine. All the tea is mine and I've earned it. Also, they are biscuits, not cookies, and I will not have this conversation again.

Perhaps the *No Soliciting* sign on my porch was confusing. Perhaps he was illiterate. Maybe I should have been more assertive in my original stance or simply not answered the door. I may never know the consequences of those other choices. Before I know its arc, my garden shovel is in my hands, in the air, and connecting with his head. A brief gurgle and then a thud. I lean my shovel against the house, my head now clear. After a respite, the morning resumes its deep breathing, as do I. Only the slightest of exhalations from the man on the ground. He'll not exhale again.

I can hear the gentle whistle of my kitchen's kettle now, and so I must turn slowly, deliberately away from my the man on the ground, who will be my soil's newest tenant, and return to my little kitchen.

I remove the kettle from the fire – the whistle dies.

We all do.

An idea starts to brew.

It's only sad to to me the man will never truly taste the bitter notes of dandelion root, nor did he stay long enough to reconcile its scent underneath the soft, wet earth - which now clings to his jacket, his cheek, and his full, quiet lips.

Through my window, I look at his body next to my flower garden – their buds and shoots quivering in the wind.

But then again, so am I.

My first cup of tea is cold now, and so it's a new cup of tea I shall drink for my second this morning. And it will be my own special blend. Judging from his size, there will be more than enough left for the coming spring days ahead.

The Beast You Bring With You
by Joe Mercer

Brian's weary gaze fell from the mesmerizing burn of the headlights and crawled back to the dusty windshield. He blinked like he had sand in his potholed eyes, yawned. "I don't remember the water being this black."

His older brother, Frank—huddled like a sack of ancient bones behind the wheel of Dad's Ford pickup—grinned. It came and went, hollow and meaningless.

Brian saw no joy in the gesture but offered a smile of his own, and immediately regretted it. It felt no less dishonest than Frank's failed attempt— a mask of awkwardness, something for his face to do, a way to hide the sorrow behind his eyes. He had lost count of how many times he did Frank the disservice of trying to relate with his suffering, trying to understand the horror of losing a child to cancer, a wife to suicide.

At least now, with Dad gone, they had something in common.

They traded the narrow bridge for a deep-rutted dirt trail, cutting east-west through a vast colorless field of bunchgrass.

Still clad in the black suit and tie he'd worn to Dad's funeral, Frank dug a Marlboro from his breast pocket. He had unceremoniously embraced the habit while his son rotted in a hospital bed. Stage four terminal lung cancer. Inoperable. Matty died six months ago, three days short of his eighth birthday.

"And for the record, I'm doing this for you," Frank said, then pointed the unlit cigarette at the cardboard box on the seat between them. "Not *him*."

"I know."

Frank lit the Marlboro, tendrils of smoke swallowing his face. Too much sorrow packed into half a year had chiseled deep lines around his mouth, stolen the brightness from his eyes. Stubble, more salt than pepper these days, darkened an otherwise pale canvas of blanched skin.

"Personally, I would've flushed the fucker down the toilet and saved us the twelve-hour drive."

Brian chuckled, hollow, just like his grin. "No…it *has* to be this way."

"Says who?"

Brian said nothing as he watched the shoreline town of Blackwater Falls evaporate in the rusted side mirror, somber and unpleasant; dark, like the clouds swarming above it. Even the autumn foliage seemed understated, the colors washed out. He found his tongue eager to stick to the gluey roof of his mouth. With a hard swallow, he hauled Dad's ashes onto his lap and hugged the box between his hands. Sixty years of life reduced to a pile of ash. At least he wouldn't be a meal for things with too many legs.

An immediate deep chill caused a strange, unpleasant stirring in his guts, like he had been eating his grandmother's stick-to-your-ribs porridge. It had the consistency of snot and tasted like sour oats and rancid fruit.

Nana…

The undeniable stench of mothballs tickled his nostrils, and the resulting sentiment was a bizarre mixture of nostalgia and trepidation. His mind slipped into the past and dug up a skeleton buried for more than thirty years. Soon the smell of mothballs was joined by the perfume of dust and mildew. Brian breathed it in, filling his lungs and head, and suddenly he was a kid again, tucked away in a closet, waiting for the old lady to find him. If he were to listen closely now, would he hear her slippers rasping on old floorboards?

"You know I always hated this fucking place, right?" Frank said, fetching Brian from the dark place his mind had dragged him. Frank's bony shoulders shrugged, then sagged. He washed his face with a hand, sighed. "Ah fuck. You were too young to know what was *really* happening."

"I get it. Trust me."

"Maybe." A bony shrug. "But you never had to sit in a canoe for eight hours watching Dad get drunk off his ass." Frank wrung the steering wheel, the worn rubber whining. "I don't know how many times I had to fish him out of the lake…"

As much as Frank hated their father, Brian knew he wouldn't say it, couldn't say it. Not today, not with his remains in a cardboard box.

You should've let him drown.

"We're here," Frank said, his brow cleaving, eyes narrowing on the windshield and the iron sign rising above the twists of oak and birch and pine, its red paint barely legible under the rust: *Madore's Lakeside Family Cabins*. He slowed the pickup to a crawl and nosed it through a breach in a collapsing post and rail fence, the truck bottoming out with a shriek. "Fucking Disneyland has nothing on this place."

Brian shifted the box on his lap. He didn't have it in him to manufacture another fake smile. "One night, that's it, okay? We have a couple beers, hit the sack, and in the morning we say our goodbyes."

Frank parked the truck and scrubbed the scruffy nub of his chin. "Like I said, we should've flushed him," he said, the cold indifference on his tone slipping like an icy blade between Brian's ribs. "I think I'm officially out of goodbyes."

"It's what Dad wanted."

"He ever gave a fuck about what we wanted?"

Brian fingered a dull corner of the cardboard lid and thought of the last time he'd seen Dad, face puckered with anguish and worry, body a cold shroud of ashen flesh draped like a dirty sheet over brittle bones.

"You weren't there when he asked," he said. "Saw what he'd become."

"Doesn't matter," Frank said, waving away the suggestion. "I still would've told him to pound salt up his ass."

"It's the least we can do."

A shrug. Simple, telling. It spoke of horrible days of hard drinking, depression, thoughts of putting an end to it all.

Nothing more to say, Brian kicked out of the

truck.

With his porridge-like guts feeling more like a brick in his stomach now, weighing him down, he started up a cobblestone lane, half expecting to hear the scrape of Nana's slippers.

***

The remains of Madore's Lakeside Family Cabins consisted of a half dozen ramshackle buildings sitting atop a rock face. Shards of charred lumber resembled the black skeletons of forgotten goliaths.

A squat, doughy figure was waiting for them in the shadows of a collapsed doorway, the sweat on his bald head shimmering in the dim blue-white glow of a battery-powered lantern.

Brian extended a hand. "You must be Arnold."

The man left the hand hanging, a sneer wringing his face like an old dish rag. "You got somethin' for me?"

"Yeah. Yeah, of course."

Brian removed an envelope from a jacket pocket and handed it over. Arnold thumbed through the five crisp bills and seemed pleased. He stuffed the cash into his jeans and tossed the envelope, a breeze ushering it away, into the dying light.

He turned toward a narrow cut in the trees. "Come on, then. I ain't got all night."

Beyond the dense knot of brush, a path snaked through a field of hip-high yellow grass. The

Madore homestead sat at the far end of the field, stark white against a canvas of darkening sky. A pitched roof sloped back from a flat front, and the bits and bobs of a gray stone chimney rose from its center. It looked nothing like the home they used to visit.

Jesus, look at this place...

They followed Arnold up the furrowed dirt laneway and across a parcel of dead grass to the front porch. He bobbed up the tired steps and went to work, removing a padlock from the front door.

"Lovely smell," Frank said. "Part jockstrap, part lunchmeat."

Arnold tossed a smirk over his shoulder. "That's rot."

"Great," Frank said. "If I don't have lung cancer already, I'm sure the black mold will take of that."

The room directly off the foyer was a perfect square, perhaps twenty by twenty, but felt much smaller than Brian remembered it. The crumbling remains of the stone fireplace looked like a toothless mouth frozen in a forever scream, the ceiling above it veined brown and sagging. All but a few hangnails of wallpaper had been stripped and strewn about the room, left to decay with the rest of the trash. A single piece of furniture, Nana's blue Victorian sofa, sat atop the carpet of refuse, balls of yellowed stuffing hemorrhaging from chew holes in the velvet. On the floor beside the sofa were a Styrofoam cooler and a rusted camping stove.

Impossible to peel back the pall of age and

neglect. It clung to the house with jagged claws and needle teeth, and Brian's mind refused to scrub away the grime, refused to place his younger self here, sitting cross-legged on the floor, drawing with crayons or playing with toy cars.

Arnold sucked air through his teeth. "As you know, the kitchen's in there," he said. "Like I told ya on the phone, don't drink the water. Shit'll make you as dumb as a bag of hammers. Or kill ya. One of the two."

Brian had Googled the organic solvent and discovered its link to bipolar disorder and schizophrenia. He wasn't at all surprised.

Arnold carried on. "The toilets ain't working though, so take your business outside. But you'll wanna stay away from the outhouse."

Frank tensed. "What's wrong with the outhouse?"

Arnold's wayward smirk widened.

"I appreciate you allowing us to stay here. It means a lot to my brother and me," Brian said, tapping the lid of the cardboard box. "We're spreading our dad's ashes down by the lake in the morning."

"I'll be back before noon to lock up," Arnold said, already turning toward the door. "Don't be here."

***

"I'm going to take a look around," Brian said as he set Dad's ashes on the splintered remains of the fireplace mantle.

"Be my guest." Frank slapped a sofa cushion, decades of dust spewing from it. "I'll be right here, food for the mites."

Ankle-deep in trash, Brian followed a cramped corridor to an alcove at the rear of the house, the blackened walls retracting from his gaze, as if mocking him, urging him deeper into the roiling gloom.

A familiar door hung on tarnished hinges, its frame battered, the raw wood showing in places where the many layers of white paint had chipped away. The corroded leftovers of a padlock latch hung loosely from the frame.

Uneasiness skittered like a silverfish across his scalp.

Don't...

Brian nudged the door open with the toe of his boot and gasped. The aroma was one of sour milk and soiled hamster cage bedding. He mashed a fist into his nose and turned from the stench, his stomach lurching. Heaved, spit.

Christ...

Eyes flush with tears, he stabbed the flashlight into the closet. The beam crawled over the dregs of a grubby crib mattress, the scraps of a fleece blanket, and a disembodied head of a doll, misshapen and missing one blue eye. Beneath the cliché murals of graffiti on the walls were the innocent scribbles of children locked away with only their thoughts and fears to keep them company.

There, amongst the scratches and swirls of color, was his name.

Brian recoiled from the sight, the entirely of his body rucking.

He could vaguely remember scrawling it, could almost feel the rock-like nub of red crayon pressed between his thumb and index finger. He made a fist, released, but the sensation remained.

Nana...

Brian imagined her skulking in the furthest corner of the closet, watching him, her haunting eyes shimmering like shards of broken mirror in the blackness. He wanted to lift the flashlight, point it at her, but could get it to rise only an inch. A whisper of light caught a knife in her right hand and shivered up the blade's edge.

'Just a taste, Peanut...Nana's soooooo hungry...'

He squeezed his eyes shut.

Get out of my head!

She crept from the shadows, gaunt, hunched and slow, the sandpaper tread of her slippers scraping the ground. Oily strips of gray hair hung like a tattered veil in front of a cadaver face. Her flesh was pale, webbed with bruises, and threaded with collapsed veins.

'I'll take just a nibble... just a piece,' she said, the promise hissing wet and thick in her throat. *'You won't miss it, my chubby whubby peanut, you've got lots to spare...'*

Brian turned from the room and the memory snapped off, as though it had been a movie playing in his skull, and hurried back to the living room.

Frank was prone on the couch, eyes closed, feet propped on a dusty arm, a Marlboro dangling from his lips, and a can of Budweiser clutched between his hands.

"You couldn't wait for me?" Brian asked.

***

At the end of an overgrown cobblestone path, a thirty-foot dock floated atop a mirror of black water.

Brian and Frank sat in Adirondack chairs, drinking shots of Jim Beam and cans of beer, smoking cigarettes, and talking nonsense. Nonsense ensured the conversation distanced itself from their father, as if they were both afraid of his ghost, afraid of digging up demons they couldn't scatter into the night with his ashes.

"When Mom told me Uncle Earl sold this place I was so fucking happy," Frank said, his eyes heavily lidded, the booze and drugs getting the better of him. "I thought I'd never have to see it again."

Brian dropped his gaze, wrung his hands, and sighed. "Frank…"

"Let me finish, let me finish." Frank took a sloppy pull from a can of Bud, reached out, and patted Brian's knee. "But this is good, man, this is *really* good. Getting to see you again, even if it has to be here…"

"It's been too long."

"You got that right."

"Like Mom always said…"

"Weddings and funerals."

"Weddings and funerals." Frank shook his

head. "Only way to get this fucking family together." He lifted his beer in a 'cheers' motion. "To the Madores...a bunch of dysfunctional assholes."

Brian snorted, beer gushing out his nose and down his shirt. "Look what you made me do, you bastard."

"Not my fault you can't hold your booze."

The conversation continued on for another four beers, carefully skirting the topic of Douglas Madore—the man, the father, the alcoholic whose darkness knew no limits, whose demons lived long after his death.

It didn't, however, stop Brian's thoughts from growing dark, heavy.

The memory of the crayon pressed against his thumb and index finger again and he gave the hand a shake, rubbed it on the thigh of jeans. Closed his eyes. In the darkness behind the lids, he spotted his spidery name scribbled amongst the madness.

Other names.

Names he knew.

Cousins, uncles, aunts.

Dad's.

Names he didn't.

He said, "Can I ask you something?"

"Yeah," Frank mumbled, coughed. He must've dozed off in the chair. "Sure."

"Did Nana ever..." Brian laughed at himself, shook his head.

"What?"

"I can't believe I'm actually asking you this."

"Spit it out."

"Did she ever…you know."

Frank knuckled the tiredness forcing his eyes to hang low. "No, I don't."

"Did she ever…hurt you?"

"Hurt me? No. Jesus Christ, Brian, the woman was a saint." He sat up in the chair and straightened his spine with a grimace. "Okay, maybe not a saint. I mean, Dad had some stories, but she never put her hands on me. Why?"

"Dad had stories? Like what?"

Frank glanced at his watch, shook his head. "No way. Too late to get into that shit."

"Did she hurt him?"

A sigh. "Where do think that scar above his eye came from?"

"I don't know. I never thought of asking."

"She threw him through a window for tracking coal dust into the kitchen."

Jesus…

New breath refused to fill Brian's lungs. He tilted his head back, bit off a gasp.

"Come on." Frank hauled himself out of the chair. "We've got a long drive in the morning."

Back at the house, Frank grabbed his pillow and sleeping bag from the floor and flopped onto the couch, a plume of dust rising around him.

"A little something to help you sleep?" he said, digging an Altoids tin from a pocket and giving it a shake.

"Do I even want to know?"

"Benefits of having a kid with cancer," he said, his drunken smile vanishing. He cleared his voice with a cough. "It's medical marijuana.

They're like Gummy Bears, but they mellow you out. Come on, try one. It won't kill you, I promise."

"I think I've had enough mind-altering chemicals tonight, thanks."

"Suit yourself." Frank popped three gummies in his mouth and pocketed the tin. He linked his fingers behind his head, laid back with a yawn, and closed his eyes. "So…that Arnold guy was one creepy motherfucker, eh?"

With that, Frank started snoring.

"So, I guess *you* get the couch then?" Brian said.

***

The first scream yanked Brian from his dreamless slumber. The second caused him to bolt upright.

The couch was empty beside him, save for Frank's pillow and tangled sleeping bag.

"Frank?"

A floorboard above his head creaked and a sprinkling of drywall dust fell around him.

Brian unzipped his sleeping bag, slipped his legs free, and stood, unsteady in the dark. His full bladder ached, his head knocked.

A piss and an Advil would have to wait.

He found his flashlight in the dark, turned it on, and approached the foot of the staircase leading to the second floor. Knifed the bright beam upward.

"Frank?"

A half minute ticked off in his head, his bladder.

Goddamn it.

Brian accepted the loose railing into his grasp and started the slow ascent up the stairs, into the darkness.

"Frank, I swear to God, if you're up there fucking around—"

A creak, a giggle.

Brian froze midstride, sucked in a lungful of stale air, choked on it.

"Frank?" The name squirted between his lips, thin and watery. He dug a fist into his side, massaging his bladder, begged it to hold on a minute or two longer. "I really gotta piss, man, so if this is some kind of a joke…"

Brian finished the short climb to the second floor, stepped onto the threadbare carpet runner, and combed the long hallway with the flashlight. In no rush to retreat, the stubborn murk lampooned the light, drawing black faces in the dark that scoffed and laughed silently.

Another giggle jangled like dry bones, muted by distance and a closed door.

The master bedroom.

Brian's light pushed through the sneering faces, trembled.

Frank?

With each of his steps, the house seemed to heave around him, as if breathing, dust falling from splits in the ceiling, dancing like moths in the flashlight beam.

He whispered Frank's name again.

The door at the end of the hall unlatched on its own and crept open with a soundless yawn, peeling back the skin of murk. Perfect blackness waited beyond the threshold.

The mild, aged scent every old house inherits wafted from the yawning black maw, shrouding Brian in its embrace. Mold and mildew, deep enough in the marrow of the walls that no amount of scrubbing would ever exorcise it.

And something else.

Mothballs and...fuck me...is that medicated cream?

With the dry tip of his tongue mashing against the back of his teeth, Brian broke free from his thoughts, and approached the open door. He refused to push deeper than the threshold, choosing instead to allow the flashlight to do his dirty work.

A shadow stirred at the center of the splash of light and crawled the wall, skulked across the ceiling, and melded with the dark—gone before Brian could track it with his flashlight.

'You shouldn't have come back.'

Brian flinched, jerking the beam from the ceiling, back to the corner. The light shuddered on the pained bleached face of a little girl.

A face he recognized.

He wheezed, braced himself against the door frame. "Meaghan...?"

His cousin stared into the light, the slick threads of her blonde hair a gleaming white shroud. Her gray flesh glistened as if wet with rot, oozing heat and nastiness. The tattered remnants of a noose hung around her neck, one frayed end looking like a woven crucifix resting at the center of her tiny chest.

Meaghan was ten years old the summer she and her four older sisters disappeared from the campground. Upon finding their overturned canoe, authorities dredged the lake over a period of three days but no bodies were found.

Brian never saw the girls nor his aunt or uncle again.

"You didn't drown…" he said, surprised by his ability to force the words past his lips. "She did this to you…didn't she? Nana."

Meaghan stepped forward, Brian stepped back.

A wisp of cold air climbed his spine and the hair on his arms responded. Someone was behind him now, in the corridor, between him and the stairs. He could feel their eyes burrowing onto his flesh like ticks, but couldn't bring himself to turn his back on the dark room, on his dead cousin.

Meaghan's lips quivered, pulling back into a grin, exposing the black splinters of rotted teeth. *'It will never let you leave.'*

An icy mouth pressed against his right ear and a chorus of tiny voices spoke at once:

'Nana, Nana, that nasty hag…the things she did would make you gag…she hung five granddaughters until they were dead…now Nana won't stop until she is fattened and fed.'

Brian whirled and bolted, scornful laughter chasing him to the head of the staircase. He glanced once toward the room, spotted Meaghan quaking with glee as the door slammed shut. He took the steps two at a time, stumbling over his concrete feet, buckling to his knees as he reached the bottom.

A head rose above the arm of the couch, tired eyes probing the dark. "The fat man was right," Frank said, half asleep. "You do not want to go into that outhouse."

"Frank…"

"What?"

"Didn't you hear that?"

Frank blinked, looked about the room. "What?"

"Jesus Christ." Brian crawled across the living room floor, collapsed beside the couch, and leaned his sweaty forehead against its tattered arm. "You really didn't hear it?"

Frank sat up, suddenly more awake. "Hear what?"

"The screaming, the laughing, the…"

"The *what?*"

Then they both heard it.

***

Brian kicked aside a knot of trash and hauled open the cellar door. A lick of stale air washed across his face, brushing back a curl of hair from his brow. It carried with it a suggestion of decay and wetness. He coughed into a fist, his eyes welling up.

"Jesus Christ, will you please wait a second?" Frank said as he came tumbling into the kitchen, struggling into his suit jacket. He glanced down the cellar steps, frowned. "You're not really thinking about going down there are you?"

The darkness at the foot of the steps was too thick to be natural, and the longer Brian stared at it, the more it moved, rippling like the black waters of a backwoods swamp.

"It started down there," Brian said, stuffing the cardboard box into a backpack and throwing a strap over his shoulder.

"What?"

"She used to chase me with a knife."

"What? Who?"

Brian met his brother's panicked stare. "Nana."

"Nana?" Frank recoiled. "You're not making any sense."

Nana, Nana, that nasty hag...

"At the end...when she'd get hungry," Brian said, the words tasting like Nana's rancid oatmeal, "she'd chase me with a knife, tell me she wanted a little taste, tell me that I had lots to spare."

"Get the fuck out of here."

Frank tried to step away but Brian grabbed him by the collar, tugged him back.

"I used to hide in a closet near the boiler," he said, hoping his brother could see the certainty in his eyes, hear the conviction of his tone. "She'd never follow me into that room. *Ever.* I think she was afraid of it. That's where I have to go. That's where it has to end."

With his hands out at his sides, braced against the exposed brick walls, insects moving in and out of cracks and crevasses and across his fingers, Brian negotiated the staircase, the old wood heaving under his feet, threatening to splinter and send them tumbling into the dark.

Frank followed, wielding a flashlight.

Brian listened intently for the tiniest of sounds —a knock or a bang or a whisper—but heard nothing over the blood pumping loudly in his ears, like a headache without the pain.

"I saw Meaghan upstairs, Nana," he said. "I saw what you did to her. I know what you did to her sisters…our cousins…I know what you did to Dad."

The walls trembled beneath his fingertips, the stairs rumbled beneath his shoes.

"You feel that?" Frank said.

Brian held up a silencing hand.

A small shape beetled in the shadows at the foot of the staircase. A little boy shape. Glittering eyes, saliva on teeth.

Frank tensed, a hot rush of air bounding from his lungs, brushing across Brian's left ear. "Tell me you saw that," he said, his harried attempts to chase the shape with the flashlight failing miserably.

"Ignore it."

Frank snorted. "What the fuck you mean, ignore it?"

"She knows we're coming for her. She's trying to scare us, see things that aren't really there."

The stairs groaned beneath them, crying out as tired nails slipped free from rotten lumber.

Frank's hand found Brian's shoulder. They both locked in place, their horrified eyes fastening together.

Brian remembered Meaghan's words.

'You shouldn't have come back. It will never let you leave.'

"Brian?"

This was a mistake.

Brian wheeled. "Go back!"

The stairs folded around them, Frank lurching forward, collapsing atop Brian, and they plummeted as one down into the dark.

***

Consciousness came to Brian much slower than his agony, like a muddy seam in a sea of mist, leaving him groggy, nauseous, and unable to distinguish between the ebbing blackout and reality. He knew the pain was real. It started at a rotten core somewhere between his left ankle and knee, radiated up his leg and into his groin, before finally settling sour and hot in his belly.

He juddered like a man dreaming of falling from a great height. The jerky movement caused painful waves to churn deeply in his right shoulder and he forgot all about the sharp stabs of pain in his leg. He cursed and pawed at his arm, hanging loose and useless beside him.

"You okay? Frank?"

Wishing away the gyrating spasms of pain failed miserably.

"I think my arm's broken. Maybe my ankle,"

Brian said and lowered his cheek to the cold dirt, breathed in dust. The cellar was quiet and without form, lost in near perfect darkness. "Frank?"

"He's down here," Frank said, voice crackling with sadness. The words sounded like they had been wrenched from his gut and thrown across the room.

"Frank! Jesus Christ." Brian craned his painful neck to search the area of darkness behind him, stretched a hand into the black. "Where are you? You okay?"

"I heard *him*. He's down here…in the dark."

Brian jerked as if Frank punched him in the sternum. "What? Who?"

"My little boy," Frank croaked, sobbed. "That was him at the bottom of the stairs. Matty. He's down here."

Matty had been a waxy corpse in a coffin the last time Brian had seen him. Chicago Cubs tee, blue jeans, Nikes. Frank had said his son hadn't worn a suit a day in his life, he wasn't about to start now.

"He's not," Brian said.

"I saw him. He spoke to me."

Brian tried to move again, wished he didn't, and coughed away a stone from his throat. "It's *her*, Frank. Nana. She's in this house, her darkness, her evil. It flows through its veins like blood. She knows…she gets inside your head and she knows--"

Eyes adjusting to the dark, Brian pulled his brother's dark gray silhouette from the gloom. "Frank, please…"

Frank moaned, fought to his feet, swayed, and clutched his head between his hands. Brian reached for him but he stepped back, screwed knuckles into his eyes.

"He's right there," Frank said, dropping his hands from his face. He blinked at the dark. "Smiling at me…"

Bones encased in fresh ice, Brian turned his neck painfully, deliberately, and followed his brother's weary gaze.

Matty stood a few feet away, close enough for Brian to reach out and snatch him by the ankle if he dared. Gone was his favorite tee and blue jeans and Brian could clearly see the angry puckered flesh surrounding the Y-incision carved into the boy's bony chest. A half-grin slanted the boy's colorless lips.

Oh Jesus.

Frank stepped over Brian, hand outstretched, trembling with aching anticipation. Brian couldn't snake his good arm free quick enough to grab hold of his brother, his fingers brushing the bottom hem of Frank's pant leg, and falling useless to the dirt.

"Frank—no!"

Matty looked up adoringly, smiled, and took his father's proffered hand. His dead gaze came back around, found Brian, and narrowed.

'We've got something special for you, too, Uncle,' the boy said and, together with his father, slinked into the dark. The yellowed whites of his eyes lingered in the gloom for an instant, then vanished. *'You'll see.'*

"Goddamn it, Frank. Frank!"

Brian pushed up onto his elbow but couldn't force himself further. He took time to refocus, to cull the unrelenting spikes of pain in his leg and shoulder. He choked up bile and let it slither down his chin. He didn't have the strength to spit.

It took him a full five minutes to get to his feet. His left ankle was badly sprained but not broken, at least not that he could tell. He was able to put some weight on it. Frank's flashlight lay amongst the staircase debris. Brian gathered it, switched it on, and gave it a shake to keep it lit. Wan light dripped from the cracked glass.

Fresh markings had been left in the dirt. Tracks. Two sets. Brian limped alongside them, diving deeper into the bowels of the old home, sweeping the beam from left to right like a blind man's cane. Although only five-eight, he was forced to duck below the exposed beams and pipes. He couldn't imagine how Frank, who was six inches taller, made it through in the dark without cracking his head.

Irrational strands of claustrophobia slowly drew taut around his mind.

"Goddamn it, Frank. Where are you?"

Brian crept deeper still, past the boiler room, his feet incredibly heavy. His legs had no feeling at all. The sensation crawled in his groin and stomach and fluttered like the powdered wings of a dying moth. Each step was exhausting. An oily skin of fresh sweat coated his flesh, clothing clinging to him. He could taste the salt on his lips, the corners of his eyes burned. He blinked hastily and wiped his brow.

His light fell upon the folds of a soiled canvas tarp hanging from the ceiling. He brushed it aside and followed the tracks through an entranceway into a new room, froze.

"Frank?"

His brother stood in the corner, his back to Brian, staring down into the remnants of a stone well, crumbs of old bricks littering the ground around his feet.

"I asked him not to go down there…" His voice was hoarse and wet from crying. "But he said…he said Nana wants to see me again…and if I follow… if *we* follow…we can be together forever."

"He's *not* down there…"

Frank removed a jackknife from a pocket and unfolded it. Thin pearl inset on a wooden handle, a wicked, almost sickle-like blade. Dad's fishing knife. Brian had tucked it away in the breast pocket of his father's suit the day of the funeral.

"Frank! Come on, man. Put that *fucking* thing away."

"Together forever. Doesn't that sound wonderful?" He stepped onto the jagged lip of the well, hesitated, looked back. His face was drawn and ashy, his cheeks muddy with dirty tears. "I can't go another day without him."

"Please…Frank…I'm begging you…please put it down."

Frank began to say something but stopped. His eyes fell and he began to sob.

"Listen to my voice, Frank. It's the *only* voice here. Whatever it is that you think you're hearing, it's not real. Okay? Please look at me. Please tell me you understand."

"I understand," Frank said, "but I don't care."

"I need you with me," Brian said, thinking of the Bic lighter in his jeans pocket, the small can of lighter fluid stashed in the cardboard box with their Dad. "I can't do this alone."

"Neither can I."

The knife came up slowly and drew across his throat, peeling back flaps of flesh and opening a spigot of blood.

"No!" Brian buckled painfully to the dirt as a stab of lightning jolted up his injured leg into his shoulder. His face met the floor with a cloud of dust and he screamed, getting a lungful of grit. "Frank!"

Frank's gaze found Brian and held firm, pain erupting in his eyes. Regret. Fear. He accepted a final gurgling breath into his lungs before collapsing, limp and lifeless, over the lip of the well.

Brian lay in the dirt a long time and cried hard until the tears dried up. Darkness stole the edges of his vision and crept silently across his eyes.

Don't care...

The waxy hairs on the back of his neck prickled as a wisp of gummy breath crawled across his skin and filled his head with a million irrational thoughts—leftovers from memories he hadn't shaken despite decades of the best therapy money could buy. Couldn't look back over his shoulder, not even a sideways glance, not now that he could so plainly smell mothballs and vinegary decay.

Boiler room…

Another breath scuttled like roaches through his sweat and he tensed, ears burning with the exasperating silence.

Brian pawed the lighter through the grubby fabric of his jeans. "Please…you've got enough," he said, his face buried in the dirt. "Just leave me alone."

'Just a taste, peanut…'

***

A cough jolted Brian awake.

He tried to sit up but his head weighed a million pounds. He pressed his palms into his eyes in an attempt to scrub away any lasting whispers of slumber, and through a mist of swirling white spots, the world around him began to sharpen. The raw hangnail twists of wallpaper. The cold yawning maw of the crumbling fireplace. The creeping yellow-brown stain on the ceiling.

A shadow darker than the rest stirred and a silver-white flash splintered the black, flickered, and then disappeared.

Brian started, his shoulders rising from the dusty sofa, his eyes growing wide on the gloom. He stared until he was able to draw the shape from the shadows.

The second oldest of Meaghan's sisters, Bridget, oozed from the dark like pus from a septic wound. A saw-toothed smile and bloodless puncture wound eyes were the only blemishes spoiling the china-like smoothness of her chalky

66

face. Not unlike Meaghan, bruises darkened the flesh beneath the smooth curve of Bridget's tiny jaw.

Oh Jesus Christ...

Brian shut his eyes, clenched his fists, and was reminded of his broken arm.

She's not real, she's not real, she's not--

'Drink.'

Brian gazed upon his cousin, tensed as nausea steamrolled him. She stood before him, a grimy glass clutched in her small hands.

"I know you're not real," he said, turning his face away from the water. "None of this is real."

'Your fever's finally broken,' a second voice said.

The eldest sister, Elizabeth, was suddenly standing at the foot of the sofa. She had been fourteen when she was murdered. Tall and slim, she shared her sisters' pastel skin and honey wheat hair and wicked bruising beneath her jaw. Her boyish form was hidden under a white cotton dress, her tiny feet bare.

Dorothy and Yvonne loitered behind her, on the edge of the shadows. Dorothy's pale blue eyes snuck to Brian's left leg and lingered, growing colder the longer she stared.

'We did the best we could with the available provisions,' Elizabeth said, sounding disappointed, perhaps embarrassed.

Brian pushed up onto his good elbow and nearly fainted as broiling agony surged through his bones. He fought through it and held himself upright, shaking from the effort. His legs were covered with a white sheet, a splotch of crimson darkening the area where his left knee should've been.

"What…is this?"

An arrangement of soiled instruments were set out beside him. His head swam with the vivid memory of a serrated blade chewing through his left thigh, and his breath left him in one ghastly rush.

"Oh Jesus…oh God."

'Careful,' Elizabeth said. *'You don't want to tear your stitches.'*

He imagined sutures failing, his inflamed flesh separating and tearing. A gush of bitter heat rolled up his body and got inside his brain. He wanted to scream but instead clenched his jaw until his teeth squeaked loudly in his ears. He fell back on the sofa, the entirety of his body dripping with new sweat.

'We wouldn't want you to bleed to death like Mom,' Bridget said, her tone sarcastic and cold as she patted the lid of the Styrofoam cooler beside the sofa.

Brian shuddered, his voice hiding from him. He tried not to think of his Aunt Donna's decayed crabapple face staring up at him from the confines of the cooler. He dug a thumb and finger into his wet eyes, screwed deeply.

Elizabeth brushed his hand away and pressed a cold cloth against his forehead. *'But don't you worry about that,'* she said. *'If you behave, it'll take only what it needs.'*

Bridget offered a sickly laugh. *'Isn't that*

right, Dorothy?'

Terror darkened Dorothy's lifeless eyes as she peered at her tiny hands. She was missing three fingers from each.

'Yes,' she said, her trifling voice quaking as her gaze jerked toward the kitchen. She stepped back from the entrance, putting her older sisters between her and the kitchen.

Brian followed her gaze but could see only darkness beyond the entryway. "What's in there? Dorothy! Please tell me what's going on. What's in there?"

She looked at him, tears welling in her eyes. *'The beast you brought with you.'*

"The what? Wait—" He grasped for her but she was out of his reach. His fingers brushed the cotton of her dress and fell to the side of the sofa, knocking the cooler on its side. The rotting remains of Aunt Donna's arm rolled onto the floor. Flies took to the air and maggots writhed on the decaying flesh. "Oh…" his voice broke in his throat. "Oh my god."

'Some always spoils,' Bridget said, cackling with amusement.

The gangrenous stench of the decaying arm was overpowered by another aroma—a more familiar, frightening bouquet. Mothballs and mildew and dust and medicated cream. Sour, like a clogged sewage drain.

The bottoms of old slippers scratched across the kitchen floor.

'Where's my chubby whubby peanut?'

The Bloodiest Forty-Seven Acres in the U.S.
by Mark Hines

I followed the plain gray prison bus for nearly four hours to get to the Missouri State Penitentiary where we were to pick up several dozen inmates and bring them back to our camp. I drove the chase car, the vehicle whose job it is to watch the ass of the bus and shoot anything not wearing blue that comes out of the doors while we were on the road. It is not a bad job, and I kind of like being on the road rather than being stuck in a housing unit wing. Just drive, jam out to Sabbath, or Floyd, or Rage Against the Machine, or whatever, and keep an ear on the mic in case the boys start getting rowdy and they have to pull over. I figure if anybody makes it out the doors they will have already fought their way past the bus driver and the officer riding shotgun, so I have no qualms about blowing away some idiot who may have already wasted a couple of my friends.

We traveled one hundred and thirty miles through windy Ozark back roads to find out that we were not going to be picking up our shipment of assholes from the area just inside the front sally port at "The Walls;" we were going to have to drive around the back and go way up inside the place. We turned around, and followed the street along the giant, twenty foot tall wall of stone topped with rickety, twisted up, corroded razor wire, past gun tower after gun tower where our bastard cousins from across the state stood looking down with weary eyes and itchy trigger fingers while holding shotguns and AR-15's. We did our grey bluebird bus riding best to traverse a street where the potholes are so bad that eventually the road gives way to crumbled chunks of stone and pavement, and then we bounced along after the street became hard packed dust down by the railroad tracks in plain sight of the Missouri River.

We followed the medieval castle wall past areas where it had fallen down into ruin during the flood of '92 -- past the stains of cleanliness created by an ungodly high water mark halfway up the wall. The flood had cleaned about a hundred years worth of pain and misery off from the stones. As we drove by I was in awe of that clearly visible line where the top portion of the wall had not been washed clean was in sharp contrast against the scum and residue of prison filth. The wall had only been built in 1918; the prison itself had been built in 1836. We continued along the wall, and came to a stygian back gate where we would be allowed to pass inside.

The back gate is right beside the railroad tracks, between two time worn gun towers that stand precariously above the tracks while trying not to fall every time a train comes by. The gate is one humongous steel door with umpteen layers of paint peeling off and a sign above them saying "Abandon ye hope, all who enter." I shit you not.

Above this sign hangs a perilous looking catwalk of rickety metal and bent wrought iron handrails where more guards stand with shotguns.

My first impression of the place after I finished saying "Holy Sheep Shit" under my breath was that it was like something out of the Mad Max trilogy. I locked my Remington 870 shotgun in the trunk, climbed onto the prison bus, and waited to ride inside while two guards pushed open first one door, then the other door of this prehistoric hellhole, allowing us to drive into the sally port where our brothers in arms would inspect our vehicle for anything out of the ordinary before we allowing us to cross into the security envelope..

The sally port was a giant concrete and steel fish tank of a holding area halfway in and halfway out of the prison, where vehicles coming in and going out are checked for stowaways and contraband before being allowed safe passage. Everywhere around us the strangest mixture of modern weaponry and defenses clashed against the background of rundown buildings that were old a century ago. From within the sally port, the only thing I could see were the officers who had a perfect line of fire from atop the catwalks. They could have blown any of us away, had they wished. There were two other gate officers: one knuckle-dragging gorilla type Gestapo motha' who was dressed in the black uniform of the Emergency Squad -- This guy would be our escort -- and a van parked outside where two Correctional Special Tactics And Response officers sat waiting for God only knows what. They were heavily armed and looking very anal-retentive.

We received safe passage through Mad Max's

back gate, and the two gate officers moved ahead of us to open another gate to whatever lay beyond the river Styx. After we came through, they pushed back the giant steel I-Beam that stretches across the sally port, making sure that the triangular shaped barricade was in place. Such a wicked defense of exists to prevent any inmates who might have beaten someone down and stolen a tractor or eighteen-wheeler from ramming the gates and trying to break free. We steered a converted blue bird prison bus down through a myriad of run down, terribly damaged buildings scarred with age and the markings of past violence. The scene was what you'd see in the ghetto if all the poor old grandmas and crack whores and pawnshop owners pulled out and just left the freaks and mutants to have at it and totally overrun the place. Jefferson City Correctional Center looked like 1970's Harlem in the wake of anybody who might still give a damn just packing up their shit and getting the hell out of dodge.

Time after time, past tributary after tributary of some Congolese native's idea of a road, I got out and helped our Colonel Kurtz looking Emergency Squad escort unlock and relock gnarled, twisted, beaten and abused excuses for metal gates. Stuck inside a bus with steel metal bars for windows, we drove deeper down winding, pothole afflicted alleyways, and had to constantly stop, maneuver, and re-maneuver the grey beast just to be able to traverse the maddening realm. Red brick buildings eight stories tall, where broken out windows with smoky stains above, where the fires of past riots stained a city's memory. Beaten and battered weight equipment chained down to asphalt -- the only semi-modern looking environmental sights to see -- served as playground equipment for criminal He-Men. Rusted and dented weights and bars were strewn about in poorly fenced in yard and recreation areas.

Every bit of pavement was horribly sunken in places, and was chipped and pitted, where it existed at all. Entire chunks of concrete and steel were just lying around, calling out to criminal minds for the chance to bash in people's skulls, or slit their throats. The rims of all the basketball goals had been either violently torn from their backboards, or were mangled in a wretched manner, frozen at sickening angles. Everywhere were layer upon layer of half-peeled paint -- on relic steel bars, and on every prehistoric portcullis. There were countless windows and doors that all been bricked up with mortar and stone decades before, repair upon repair, until finally many Iron Barred doorways had just been welded shut, and bricked up with even more mortar and stone. This place reeked of Poe and Lovecraft.

Everywhere there was an ominous sense of something more horrible than the fear, anger and pain of the "not that bad" prison life that I knew after working three other maximum security prisons. Here was flesh that rotted even as it walked. Here there was an eerie siphoning of life's essence away from the hearts of men, down, far down, into a hellish quagmire of some dark and sinister spiritual abyss. There were miserable ghosts so formidable they lived for centuries in those many unmapped corners where the light never reached. I had been told on numerous occasions by guards who had the misfortune of having worked in this place that were entire unexplored dungeons beneath the surface of this Kafkaesque dreamscape. Some guards had been unlucky enough to get lost down in there; there were no maps – no one knew how far down the catacombs extended. Everyone told stories of missing bodies, and severed heads, and shit so crazy that it just didn't sound real until you actually had the chance to see that maybe the place was uglier on the inside than it looked on the outside.

There was an undercity not on any of the five different known blueprints that exist for the place. In this prison, the first to built west of the Mississippi River less than a decade after Louis and Clark returned from their trek out west, there lurked an oily, slick, "hanging in the air" sort of evil. At other prisons, a man can feel it slide across his para-sympathetic nervous system, and even see it eat at the floodlights at night, but here… Whatever this spiritual miasma was, it was strong enough to eat away at your heart in broad daylight. It did not surprise me at all that many of the more superstitious inmates who had passed through the ancient prison believed that down there, deep in the crumbling, walled off ruin, there were places where the undead shambled among the deepest, darkest shadows.

On the way up through the heart of "The

Walls" I had asked our Emergency Squad escort why all the paranoia. I had been on the Squad for two years at a previous institution, and I knew that the only way the JCCC Emergency Squad would have been activated was if they expected shit to kick off.

"Around here we always plan for the worst, because nine times out of ten, the worst happens," Our black uniformed Sergeant answered.

They expected shit to kick off. They'd had another guy get hacked up into pieces and they found him frozen in the icehouse, a couple of days before. Two inmates were unaccounted for, had been for going on three days at this point, and were holed up somewhere within the catacombs, most likely with a store of food and a few homemade weapons. The Overlords of the Underworld would have their hypothesis proven for them a month later when someone wandering around in places they shouldn't have been stumbled onto the "escaped" convicts by chance, and somehow managed to get away without being cut into bite sized chunks of meat.

When we arrived at our objective – An unnumbered, unnamed house of pain -- nearly two dozen other E-squad members and even two teams of Corrections Special Tactics and Response met us. All of these guys were pretty hard core. Every one of them had shaved heads, or virtually no hair. Mean motherfuckers, all dressed in black battle dress uniforms and sporting H-harnesses, Tac vests, gas masks, and thigh holsters. A few even had concussions grenades and MK-9's (Pepper

Spray that comes in a can the size of a liter bottle mountain dew) strapped in pairs to their chests. These people were not fucking around.

We entered the Ninth circle. It was a seven story, red brick building where the tiers of cells stood so high that one had to crane one's neck back as far back as it could go, just to see the ceiling. Far beneath the fraying tiles of asbestos stained by the smoke of fires, there was, down in the floor of the cell block, a swamp of stagnant water in the center bay. The floor of the bay was about six inches lower than the floors of the cells, and the floors of the cells were slightly sloped to allow the filth to drain into the center of the cell block.

There were pieces of scrap paper, cardboard, half burned trash, and rotting chunks of identified meat looking material out there in the middle of the watery floor. The slick scum of water tainted by unwashed human bodies painted oily rainbows on the surface of what all who entered had to walk through day after day. The Catwalks on each tier looked like certain death for any guard stupid enough to be caught walking on them alone and outnumbered: They were tied together into some freakish semblance of half-assed sturdiness by mangled, beaten hurricane fencing rising from the lowermost railing to the ceiling. Such had been placed there in order to prevent the inmates from throwing guards and other enemies over the railing, to gruesome deaths below. Such deaths were not unheard of – I had heard tales from nearly every guard lucky enough to be re-assigned away from "The Walls," of inmates throwing one another off of the catwalks to be maimed and sometimes killed when their bodies hit the floor three, four, even five stories down.

The cell doors were ancient steel barriers, portcullis looking constructions made of metal rusty enough to give a man tetanus just from brushing against one. They were all operated by levers and pulleys, and were not three feet from the railing, so the guards had nowhere to go if an inmate tried to grab them and cut them up. There was nowhere to go. Knives could lash out and catch a guard in the gut at any time, and there are rarely any weapons carried inside the security envelope of the prison itself, just in case there is a rebellion. The inmates owned this place. Like all prisons in this state, the typical guards only carry a radio to call for help, a small can of pepper spray worth slowing ONE guy down if you can react faster than he can and get the spray in his eyes. Aside from that, all we've got to fight back with is a pair of handcuffs – They tend to be more useful as a set of makeshift brass knuckles in a place this hostile. In any maximum security prison that can of pepper spray is not worth much in a fight where more than two or three inmates are involved. In a place like "The Walls," you are much better off using whatever improvised weaponry you can find when (not IF) you have to fight back, and hope to find a sympathetic jury should you come out of it. The good news is: If the inmates cut you up bad enough, the state sometimes guarantees a maimed guard a job for life – No matter what the fuck you do, or how bad you screw up, they promise you in writing never to fire you, just as long as you promise not to break the state treasury by suing the Department for a "hostile work environment."

We loaded up a shitload of the most bohemian, dreadlock wearing, swastika tattooed, scarred up, burnt down, bad karma dripping freaks of nature who had ever been into our bus, put a lid on the beast, and got the hell out of there as fast as we could. We had guys whose faces had been melted away by having heated bleach mixed with shaving powder thrown in their faces during fights. We had guys who had more scars from bullet holes than some kids have pimples. We had dudes on that bus so psychotic that the look in their eyes told you there was no man left inside, just the blind rage of a mad dog who in his lifetime had been poked with too damn many sticks.

There are way too many stories to tell about "The Walls." Every officer I ever met who had worked there was a sadistic motherfucker. I never knew a single guard who came from that place (once named "The Bloodiest Forty-Seven Acres in the United States,") and who lasted more than six months, who wasn't prior Army elite or USMC. Civilian officers just do not make it. Every inmate I ever knew who came out of that shithole was without conscience, and far beyond hope of rehabilitation. JCCC, "The Walls," MSP, or whatever name you are unfortunate enough know it by, the more you know about it, the less you ever want to go there. In skinhead circles, the very tattoo of those stone walls and those towers is considered sacred. To have that tattoo and to have done time there gets one tremendous respect, especially if you are an old head who was there during the eighties. Back then racial tensions were very bad, and the in-prison crimes were abnormally heinous. To have that tattoo and never have been there will get your ass stabbed, at the very least, for lying. The place is so decrepit that the guards are told not to drink the water, and the inmates have to boil their own water and let it cool before they drink it, or they will catch crazy shit that makes them sick enough that sometimes they die from it.

Every Tuesday and every Thursday it is the same thing: Men in orange jumpsuits, all of them restrained in chains, stagger around everywhere in the receiving area of the oldest prison west of the Mississippi River. Deep within this pit, twice a week, hundreds of inmates step off of bus after bus, from every institution in the state. We swap and trade their bodies like kids trade baseball cards. The inmates get off from one bus, have their identities confirmed, and then they all step back onto any one of a dozen other drab grey busses with bars on the windows and "DOC" on the side. The buses head out for the next stop at any one of this state's twenty-seven prisons.

The drive to get to this modern day slave market was always four hours long. On this day we had sixty-nine to give up, and seventy-three to bring home. We traded burglars and parole violators for murderers and serial rapists. We had our lists, and were on a schedule. There were black faces, white faces, scarred faces, angry faces, dead faces; every one of them a number for a name. Tattoos were the predominant sign of their personalities, and among themselves they knew each other only by their nicknames: "Smooth," "Lunch Meat," "Gorilla," "Cornbread," "Fee-fee," and so on.

Every Tuesday and Thursday we guards used any down time we had to catch up with old friends from different camps who we hadn't seen in ages. The buses came, gathering in the oldest, mother prison, and after twenty-seven other prisons worth of dregs from the underworld were traded, we gathered up all of our bad boys, the buses went, and we began the long journey back across the state of Missouri to whatever new prisons the criminals would soon call home. They would kick and howl and scream, and we would just turn up the most redneck country music station we could find in order to drown out their ghetto bebop with our redneck racket. They would kick the steel doors between the driver and the rodeo going on in the back. They would threaten to piss on us through the gap in the door, and I've even known a few guys to try: These fucks get pepper sprayed in the dick – No arguing, no bullshit-- If you let one asshole piss on you, then they all want to do something like it just to one-up each other. We would crank up the air conditioning until they get so cold that they would have to shut up and huddle down in their seats in order to stay warm. We would get home to our own local prisons, unload the ragged bastards, categorize them, photograph scars and tattoos, then put them into little concrete boxes and teach 'em how to do hard time.

Most of the time I would manage to get dibs on the chase car instead of having to ride in the bus on the way home. I would ride behind the bus, listening to AC /DC while driving a car that I know for a fact will do 120 mph easy, and watch the scenery fall away to the sides and then the rear. I remember pondering the strangeness of being paid to carry a loaded firearm in public and being allowed to disobey stop signs and red lights (with caution) so that nothing came between me and my bus. Those were the good days. The rest of the time, I had to sit in the jump seat of the bus itself -- That always makes for a bad day.

I'd sit listening to the howling of the animal-men, and they would kick and claw everything metal that they could while threatening, and cursing, and there was no stopping for anything – If you did, it invited a riot right there on the fucking roadway. If you had to mace one of them, it just meant that you were in for a really shitty ride in a lurching bus full of crazies all the way home. A four hour drive with pepper spray fumes to compound it all really sucks, but it sucks worse to get spit on and pissed at and to have to just sit there and take it when you know damn good and well that you don't want to. No one is going to stop fucking with you if you do just take it -- So instead of asking for respect, it is almost always just better to send any grief the inmates throw at you right back at them ten-fold. Karma is a cold-

hearted son of a bitch; sometimes that is just what
it takes to get home in one piece.

The Hunt
by Fred588

Still a half-hour or more from dawn, Wade had been on the road for nearly three hours. A cold fog filled all the low spots in the fields and filtered through intermittent, but increasingly larger, patches of forest on either side of the road. The landscape was eerily illuminated by a now setting full moon just above the western horizon. Every leaf, every blade of grass was coated with newly formed dew that sparkled and glistened like billions of diamonds when the light was just right. Part of the scene seemed appropriate to the late October season, and part of it seemed more Christmas like.

Up ahead another mile or so was a dim glow from what were probably the only artificial lights within twenty miles, other than his own headlights. The lights were those of Woody's Pit Stop, a combination gasoline station, donut shop, convenience store, and taxidermist; the only outpost of civilization within twenty miles or more in any direction.

Pulling in to the gas pump, Wade jumped out of his pickup, then quickly retreated back in to put on his heavy hunting jacket. He had forgotten how cold it could be this early in the morning. Getting out again, he unscrewed the gas cap, dropped in the regular, unleaded nozzle, and started the pump. Then, leaving the gas pumping, he went inside to Woody's.

Woody himself was manning the counter. He

was dozing as Wade entered but woke up quickly in response to the jangle of a tangle of bells hanging on the door.

"Ah ha! Sleeping on the job! I caught you!" said Wade boisterously.

"Wade P. Tidwell. What the hell are you doing out of bed at this hour? Must be your annual sorry excuse for a hunting trip," answered Woody.

"Of course, it's my annual hunting trip," Wade fired back, "I sure didn't come all the way out twenty miles past nowhere to see you're ugly face."

"That's right, give me a hard time," Woody retorted. "Enjoy yourself. Tell me all about the big buck you ain't gonna get. Talk big, cause you sure don't know nothing about hunting."

"We'll see about that," laughed Wade. "How's the hunting been around here anyway."

"Depends on where you're going."

"Tanglewood Flats. I heard they stocked it a few years ago. Some deer that were genetically engineered or something so they'd grow bigger and developed a better rack," said Wade, trying to sound as if he knew what genetically engineered meant.

"True!" said Woody. "The place is swarming with deer all year, although they do seem to disappear about now. I think they engineered them to know about hunting season too" he continued laughing.

"They say that everywhere," answered Wade. "But they have to be out there somewhere."

"Really, they're just migrating to find better

food sources for the winter," said Woody. "Still, we have had some trouble down in the Flats. A lot of hunters are staying away from that area, so there ought to be some real trophies."

"What kind of trouble?" asked Wade.

"Oh, they found some hunter's truck abandoned down there, but no hunter. Last year and the year before too," answered Wade.

"Really, what happened?"

"Oh, I don't know. Some folks think they got lost. One real paranoid guy I know thinks the animal rights people are behind it. I think the guys just needed to disappear. Alimony problems probably, so they just went hunting as a cover story and ran away," Woody explained. "Guys go hunting down there for three or four days at a time sometimes. By the time anyone starts looking for them they could be in South America," he continued.

"Two years in a row?" Wade asked.

"Why not? The second one was probably a copy cat," answered Woody, though it does seem a bit odd to happen in almost exactly the same place."

Wade pulled a six pack out of the cooler and a couple of bags of jerky off a rack near the checkout. "This and the gas will be all I need this morning. I might drop by tonight on my way home, he said. "Just to make you jealous of my trophy buck."

"Eighteen seventy-seven," said Woody, totaling the bill.

"There's twenty," said Wade, dropping two

tens on the counter.

"And there's a dollar twenty three in change," said Woody. "I'd count it out for you but I know you couldn't tell if I was lying or counting it right."

"Yeah, right," said Wade. "You wouldn't know how much to give me if the register didn't tell you."

"See you later," they both said at once as Wade went out the door.

***

The sun was just a few minutes rise above the horizon when Wade pulled off the main road onto the dirt track that led another couple of miles into the Tanglewood Flats. The Flats were eighty or so square miles of old growth forest, thickets of lush undergrowth, and other virgin wilderness inhabited only by wildlife and a very occasional hunter.

After about two miles, when the dirt track just faded out of existence, Wade stopped. Gathering his new rifle, pack containing lunch and emergency supplies, six pack, water bottle, and a few other things, he headed into the woods, full of anticipation. After a few hundred yards he selected a spot on a slight rise overlooking a clearing with a dense wood beyond. The clearing would give him a clear few of any deer venturing out of the thick brush to get at the more abundant foliage of the clearing. He sat on a fallen log just in front of a pair of very large paper birch trees, one of which was marked by a curious pair of parallel, diagonal gouges, one a couple of seasons old and well healed over; the other also healed but more recent.

For the next six hours or so Wade waited, had a beer, waited, ate his lunch and some of the jerky, waited, had another beer, and waited some more. There was no sign of any deer.

About two in the afternoon Wad had just finished a third beer, and was about to open a fourth when suddenly there was a very subtle crack of a twig from across the clearing. He looked up and squinted slightly. Across the clearing, a few dozen yards out of the effective range of his rifle, was his quarry.

And it wasn't just any deer. This one was a trophy, with the biggest, most complex rack of antlers Wade had ever seen in the wild or even in a museum.

"Whoa!" Wade said to himself very softly.

Very, very slowly and carefully Wade extended his arm to the rifle propped against the tree to his left. The deer was out of range but he wanted to be ready.

Wade's heart raced. This was a real trophy buck; one his hunting friends would talk about with envy for years. All he needed now was for the buck to move a few yards closer and one, good, careful shot.

He had all the advantage. The wind was in his face, so it carried his human scent away from the target in front of him. The sun was at his back and therefore in the buck's eyes if it should look in his direction. Although the buck was still partially concealed by brush, a few steps in the right

88

direction would bring it into the open.

Fifteen minutes went by. The trophy buck moved around, nibbled at various leaves, and seemed oblivious to Wade's presence, but it did not move within range.

Thirty minutes passed.

Forty-five minutes passed. The big buck moved tantalizingly close, but not close enough. Then, it began to move, a little at a time, but in the opposite direction.

The most magnificent buck Wade had ever seen was giving Wade a challenge worthy of the trophy he might become. But now the chance to win that trophy was slipping away.

"Okay," Wade said to himself. "What choice do I have. I'll try stalking you."

Crouching as low as he could and trying to stay behind the concealment of foliage as much as possible without losing sight of his quarry, Wade began moving forward. He moved very deliberately, one careful step at a time. He advanced to the edge of the clearing that stood between himself and the big buck. Almost step for step, the buck maintained the distance between the two of them.

"You're a wary SOB, aren't you," Wade said softly, more to himself than to the buck. "Well, I guess you don't live long enough to grow a rack like you have without being careful."

One step at a time, or sometimes in quick bursts of a few steps, Wade stalked his trophy. He worked his way around the clearing and into deeper forest on its far side. As he moved, the deer moved, always in the opposite direction. Wade reasoned that the deer was just moving away from the now lowering sun, perhaps instinctively knowing a predator would approach out of the sun, as Wade was doing. The two of them moved slowly and more or less in tandem through the dense forest, across a clearing where a fire had occurred a few years before, down an embankment, and around the edge of a pond.

On a couple of occasions Wade was able to close the range enough to get an effective shot, but each time he tried to take aim his prey moved behind a screen of brush or a tree trunk. By the time he had a relatively clear view of the deer it had again moved out of range.

Wade stalked the deer all afternoon, never quite getting close enough to risk a shot. One shot, after all, was all he would get. If he fired and missed, the trophy buck would bolt and be long gone before another shot could be prepared. Wade was not so unsporting a hunter as to use anything other than a single shot weapon. The stalk moved across a grassy field, up and over an evergreen-covered hill, and through a thicket of dense juniper bushes to the edge of an open marsh.

The marsh was more open country in which the freedom from visual obstructions would permit an effective shot to be made from a somewhat greater distance. At the same time, much of the marsh was thick with chest-high grass that could provide a crouching hunter with excellent cover while approaching a target. If he did not make a mistake, Wade knew this was where he should be able to finally bring down his elusive target. Yet, the deer was still at the extreme limit of the range at which he was sure of a kill.

Wade moved forward. The deer matched his movement. He moved again, faster this time. The deer did the same.

"Dammit!" said Wade. "Hold still for a minute."

Reaching another small clearing, Wade crouched so as to remain concealed below the top of the grass and dashed across to the cover on the far side. The deer moved similarly and matched Wade step for step as he stalked through the grass.

"Unbelievable!" Wade exclaimed to himself. "Its as if you're playing with me."

Reaching another clearing, Wade crouched again and moved forward quickly. Halfway across, however, he suddenly slipped on a patch of very slick mud. Stumbling and falling, Wade dropped the rifle and threw his arms forward so as to break his fall. Expecting a hard impact, he was startled as his arms plunged into soft mud.

"Oobbb!"

Wade's startled cry was stifled as the soft mud caught him flush in the face.

He pushed his arms down into the ooze to lift his face clear of the muck and drew his legs underneath to right himself. As he attempted to stand he was stunned as his legs just drove down into the soft mud, leaving him waist deep. This was something he had no idea how to handle. He panicked and tried to lunge forward. Though he was able to move a few feet forward, this only made things worse. The mud grew softer and deeper and the roots of various plants seemed to entangle his legs. In seconds he was chest deep and completely stuck.

As the sun began to set, Wade struggled hopelessly against the mud that was now up to his shoulders. He wasn't sinking any deeper but there seemed to be no way out of the mire. And it was getting very cold. By the time the moon was the only remaining source of light, Wade knew he would not survive the night. He was rapidly sinking into hypothermia. He made one last attempt to struggle forward and escape from the terrible grip of the mire, but it was no use. In his struggles in the darkness his hand struck what seemed to be a solid object. He grabbed it and pulled it to the surface. His eyes went wide with horror and he recognized the object as a human skull. Then he passed out. Shortly after midnight, Wade's heart stopped beating.

***

Wade's pickup truck was found by the police a few days later. Dogs were used to search the area, but the trail was lost at the top of an overlook at the base of two very large birch trees. The police detectives noted, but could not make any sense, of three parallel, diagonal gouge marks in the trunk of one of the trees, one old and well healed over, one healed over but not as old, and one quite fresh.

The Stranger
by Pete Chiarella

My life is a disaster.
Driving through a squall of snow. Renting a cabin for the weekend, in a desolate area of Kentucky, the need came.

The need to be alone, for a forest's solitude, to think things through.

How could a supposedly loving five year relationship just end? We hadn't made love in over a year. Time just … passed. What was once a life built on burning passions had turned into a pile of stale, smoky embers.

More needs came. The need to be away from friends, from the thick of it all, alone with the questions which have no answers and the thoughts that come unbidden, uncontained.

The eternal question-why. Why did he just pull away, dashing all hopes and dreams? He *needed space*, he'd said. Space for what? Why wouldn't he talk, tell me what was wrong? No, he just decided on his own he didn't want to be together any longer. And once gone, you left me a flailing, raw nerve. So I had to get away, too, and leave a place once warm with love, now cold as the snow swirling around this car.

Snow continues to fall-the cabin just ahead. Shutting off the engine, wishing to power down the surge of internal dialogue. No chance.

The owner thoughtfully left a pile of firewood by the door. Hauling bags, leaving bags just inside the door. All the things of a life least lived, brought in for the weekend. Things and thoughts. Thoughts and things. Start a fire, open a bottle of wine. The cabin starts to warm, the small windows flecked with ice. Night falls, fire crackles, look out the windows.

A baleful, full moon casts light on a snowy scene. The skeletal branches of trees reach up like hands, grabbing for something, for nothing. Gazing out at a cold, desolate landscape, almost trapped, but not quite. No love, no warmth, just emptiness. The cabin grows warmer still. Ice crystals continue to form, freeze on the windows, and a silky set of lingerie beckons. Dressing in the tainted garments, memories of lost passion emerge, threaten to consume. Fingers dip into panties, thoughts blur at the memory of what once was. Fingers continue to move quickly, decisively.

A shattering orgasm rips through, body and a few tears. Along with a thin sheen of sweat, a trickle of moisture runs down this spine, pooling at the waistband of my panties. I sense his presence before I see him. Someone on the edge of the property, just slightly out of view. He is a dark, featureless figure. Tall, gaunt and waiting for something. Unlock the door. Sit on the edge of the bed and wait. The wait is not long.

He enters the room, my sanctuary, and a numbing wave radiates from his body. He smells of old leather, gunpowder and wears a leather duster. He walks toward me, his hand lifts my chin, and I stare into his pale hazel eyes, world weary, yet kind. A kiss, long and deep, shatters my remaining soul. Panties hanging off an ankle, hot breath making everything wet with passion and desire. His probing tongue sets off explosions of orgasmic pleasure.

I must have him, no- need is the right word.

Like a hot knife though butter, he enters. I moan, as he slowly thrusts, my hands wrap behind him, and pull him deeper inside.

"More," my voice mutters, as if from far away and someone else.

"I need more." He obliges, thrusting harder, faster, the sweat pours from my body, plastering hair to scalp. Climax approaching, and it is a deluge, a seemingly endless, shaking orgasm. He's also getting close to the edge. I pull him out, take him in my mouth. He explodes and I drink every drop of his essence.

Drained, exhausted, but more alive than ever have before, I nestle in his arms and fall asleep. Contented, whole again, the world is … mine. Yours. Ours.

Fitful sleep, awakening to the sun streaming through glazed ice patterns on windows. Turning, reaching for him, but he is gone. *Where?* I question. Then I see. Footprints in fresh snow.

Dressing quickly, noting the footprints leading away from the house. Following them to the woods. They lead to a small path though the trees. *Could he have a cabin around here?* The path leads deeper into the woods, following, and it ends at an old cemetery. The footprints continue. A bit of fear bites, but I need an answer. The prints lead to an old grave, then vanish. The worn headstone reads:

Jeremiah Tidball 1841-1863
Hero of the Confederacy

Kneeling before the grave, senses reeling.
"It just can't be."
But then reality sets in. It did happen.
Attention drawn to something written in the fresh snow.
"Real love never dies." The initials JT next to it.
Standing, weak and flushed in the cold, the long walk back to the cabin, where the scent of the night still lingers. Starting to pack again, with every intention of getting away, remembering how good it was, the touch of a stranger. Sometimes they come back. I stop packing, open another bottle of wine, and look out into the day and wait for the night to fall again.

The Number of the Swan
By Barry Parsons

"All art is the result of one's having been in danger of having gone through an experience all the way to the end when no one can go any further. This is what it is like to be an artist – you are unsteady on the edge of life like a swan before an anxious launching of himself on the floods where he is gently caught." -Edmund de Waal

A once in a lifetime hunt. I had the privileged invitation when I first became a German hunter. In Germany, hunting is not for the hunter-but rather for species and environmental welfare. As a German hunter the animals taken during the hunt do not belong to you, they belong to the revere to be sold off for land maintenance and overall animal preservation.

Each May, we stop hunting and count populations. With this census, the German federal land managers develop the harvest plans for each revere; this plan dictates the number type and gender of the animals to be harvested on any given revere. Europeans learned long ago that as humans moved in and started to control the environment, the predatory species moved away. Mother Nature abhors a vacuum and will take steps to bring balance to her dominion; moreover, She can be the cruelest of huntresses with her instruments of starvation and pestilence and it is She, ultimately, who controls the populations of both human and animal. The Germans came to understand this intuitively, then mathematically, and the base nature of man's predatory desires developed a culture that helps to achieve the balance nature desires. Using modern tools and training the German hunter is the predator controlling populations as humanely as possible.

I became a German Jäger in 2010 and was invited to become a neu Jäger on a small revere in the Rheinland Phaltz district of Germany. One day the Jäger Meister Olaf Klein called a meeting of Jägers at the local gaust haus, the topic to set plans for our revere owner's 71st birthday. After much deliberation, it was settled-we would send owner Herr Klevecheski on a goose hunt. Herr Klien was able to find a hunt in northern Germany that all of us could join. He found a flieg revere owner who needed help with filling his shoot plan. Therefore, we all put our money in for Herr Klevecheski and ourselves. It was a four-day bird hunt in a small town near Hanover, with no game fees and an unlimited take as long as we stayed and ate in the flieg revere owner's gaust haus.

Arriving Wednesday night and after introductions with a touch of German hospitality, we went straight to bed for an early rise. Our first hunt began at 4:30am, with breakfast and a briefing on logistics before departure. The instructions for the day were quite simple: *if it flies, it dies*. We were told the revere was behind on its shoot plan for the year and we were there to help catch up.

We moved to our hunting points just before sunrise; it was the perfect morning to be hunting geese-cold, overcast, and raining. The clouds were low enough to keep the birds within shotgun range, but high enough to remain part of their flight plan. I was the new hunter, the youngest of the group, and found myself at the worst of all the points. It was not really hunting blind so much as a spot in a ditch. The spot wasn't all terrible. There was a lake on the other side of some reeds about 30 meters directly behind me, thus if there were any geese on the lake I could have found a shot. In hindsight, I   realize the reason I was in that particular spot: to make sure the birds would fly towards my revere owner's true blind. Geese and ducks have tremendous eyesight. They see color and movement extremely well and with me placed and exposed, they would see me and fly towards the river where the other hunters were in true blinds.

Just after sun up, for the first time in my life, I observed a million geese flock which looked like a dark cloud on the horizon. I heard the flock before I saw it, the sound similar to a concerto of people, a multitude of voices all mingling at once. Five minutes after the flock's appearance, geese started to circle our field. As I expected, they flew high in my area and started landing towards the other hunters at the opposite end of the field. The flieg revere owner instructed us not to shoot at these advance geese, because flocks as big as this one, send out individuals, scouting for a safe place to feed. The main flock finally arrived at our field at about 30 minutes after sun up and many geese started to land in the field. With so many geese around, we harvested a total that day of 20 and even I had three of those. During that hectic time, I heard what I thought was a number of very large geese taking off from the lake, so I began tracking them with my shotgun through the reeds. Just as they rose above the reeds I realized they were not geese but swans and let them go on their way. Once the flock of geese moved on we left the field for the day, and went to take a lunchbreak. The afternoon was also filled with a rabbit hunt in which we all harvested one.

At the hunter's dinner that evening, I brought up the swans taking off, and that I let them go. The flieg revere owner became upset with me for doing so, and he told me they were on his shoot plan and must be taken as he was behind his quota for them. At that point, my revere owner came to my rescue explaining that the swan is verboten in the Rheinland Pfaltz and a hunter will lose his license for shooting them. I promised them both I would shoot if opportunity presented itself again. The flieg revere owner said not likely, because they would not return for some time.

The next morning, we were up at 4:30am taking breakfast and again our instructions were *if it flies it dies*. So once more, we moved to our positions and I was assigned the same little ditch now filled with rainwater. As anticipated, the geese flock arrived on the horizon and brought with it hectic shooting. Again the sound of heavy birds taking off from the lake were heard over the fray, and I started tracking their flight path through the reeds as before. Instead of taking off parallel with the reeds, the swans were angled to take off over them, coming closer to my position so I prepared to fire. I had the perfect lead on the first swan, and waiting for them to clear the water and at the closest point to me I pulled my trigger, felt the recoil of the shotgun, and watched as the lead swan fell to earth. The swan was as big as a Reh deer and it turned out to weigh 37 kilos (81.5 lbs), and because of the muddy field I had a very long walk back to the trucks. That day I not only took the swan but took two more geese and a duck. However, that afternoon's later, additional pheasant hunt yielded no results for me.

The evening's dinner saw the flieg revere owner overjoyed with the harvesting of the swan. He further explained swans are hard to take because of their down feathers being so thick that shots bounce off them. When I dressed the swan the majority of shot was to the head, and so a quick and clean harvest. Because of the high status of the swan in the German hunting tradition, I was the Koenig of the hunt that weekend. Because of the amount of meat I harvested, I played my part and forced as many birds as possible to the others. The group was so successful in filling the shoot plan for the flieg revere owner, he invited us back the following year for the same type of hunt.

I came to understand the honor and recognition presented to me when I became a German Jäger. There are two types of American Jägers in Germany: there are those who hunt as Americans in Germany, and there are those who hunt as a German Jäger accepting and honoring their traditions and rituals. I was able to do the latter. It was such a remarkable experience going on hunts with not a word of English spoken and being knighted into the sacred order of Saint Hubertus in front of a roomful of true Jägers and Jäger Meisters. I considered my revere owner my Jagdt Pester (hunting father) and as close to me as my natural father; I recognized the prestige they bestowed upon me, and each year I was there I hosted a Jäger dinner where I supplied all the meat from some of the game I personally took that year. After the initial bird hunt in northern Germany, we had the swan at our table for the next two Jäger dinners I hosted. And it tasted like no other bird before or since.

CONTRIBUTORS

Dr. Rhonda Baughman is a new witch and an old goddess (probably a Nut incarnation), a cranky X/Y hybrid (xennenial) and the creator of MC. She is in touch with something very, very powerful, too-so, try not not piss her off. She has a 17 page writing resume that spans 24 years and two continents and she is damn proud of it. Recent pieces have appeared in Grindhouse Purgatory and Exploitation Nation. Support her Patreon: drbaughman or Reach out to her email: rhondabaughman@hotmail.com – she'll probably dig it. And if she doesn't – well, she'll give you a head start.

Jaime Bunnell is a crafty bitch. They are equal parts nerd, painter, seamstress, reader, and writer. Jaime explores the complexities of life within the LGBT community through fiction, poetry, and art. Bitch may be an exaggeration; they would say Goddexx is a much better description. Jaime lives in middle America with their spouse, kids, and doggies. They can be reached on Twitter and Instagram: @jaimebeez, or good old fashioned email: jaimebeez@gmail.com

Pete Chiarella aka *42nd Street Pete*, born on the wrong side of time and hung like a bear. He smells a little like one, too – but that stench is his love for the beast. He graduated from the School of Hard

Knocks, Class of '70, Writer, Producer, Actor, Animal Activist and Advocate for Women's and LGBTQ Rights. Creator of Grindhouse Purgatory and 8mm Madness. Has written for Chiller Theatre, Something Weird Blue Book, Uncut, Shock Cinema, Ultraviolent, Horror Biz and Screw Magazines. Wrote and appeared in Unconventional and Pollen. Email Dr. Baughman – she'll pass on your memo.

Fred 588 represents the best of the wilds of Arkansas. His story has been posted several times over the years at quicksandfans.com and at an earlier site called deepsinking.com.

Mike Hammer is a 40-year-old resident of Cleveland, Ohio. He studied Creative Writing at Bowling Green State University in Bowling Green, Ohio. Hammer is a freelance writer and marketing specialist who was born in Pittsburgh and lived in Greensboro, NC, New Orleans, Cleveland and Toledo, OH. He likes to read and attend plays and concerts.
Contact him at: mikey.hammer@gmail.com

Mark Hines was born to an alligator wrestling Cajun in the swamps of Louisiana. In his childhood, he was raised by wolves among the Bannock and Shoshone of the Fort Hall Reservation near Pocatello, Idaho, and by the Nez Perce of Eastern Oregon. He emerged from an impoverished adolescence in the Missouri Ozark hills, and grew to adulthood while working in the mental institutions and prisons of the Midwest. In recent years, he has given up making machine guns for a living while dwelling in a little house on the prairie, and awaiting the apocalypse with survivalists. He now works with the homeless in his free time, and spends his happiest moments as a recovering Neo-con frolicking among the Alpine wildflowers of the Colorado Rockies, singing show tunes, and fantasizing of the day when every member of Rage Against the Machine stomps the shit out of Paul Ryan onstage while his fortune is redistributed to the working class, and the doors of America's universities are opened to all, free of charge. Email Dr. Baughman – she'll pass on your memo.

Scott Mayer is an observer, father, lover of life, widow, actor, mixed media creator, and Renaissance Man. He lives and breathes Los Angeles. Email Dr. Baughman – she'll pass on your memo.

Joe Mercer is a former award-winning journalist who now works as a Communications Specialist for an upper-tier municipal government in the snowy wilds of Canada. He lives with two daughters, his partner Vanessa, and the monsters he keeps locked in the basement. Having recently finished writing his first novel, *Walk Me to the Darkness*, Mercer has turned his focus toward short stories. Email Dr. Baughman – she'll pass on your memo.

Barry Parsons represents the best of Colorado. Email Dr. Baughman – she'll pass on your memo.

Mike Polnik is currently defending Canton, OH. Email Dr. Baughman – she'll pass on your memo.

#fuckinmemos